I0575505

Since Day One

Abigail Nadine

Since Day One

One

A novella

Abigail Nadine

Abigail
NADINE BOOKS

For permission requests, contact Abigail Nadine at abigailnadinebooks@gmail.com.

Title: Since Day One / Abigail Nadine
Description: Abigail Nadine Books, 2025
Identifiers: ISBN: 979-8-9988104-2-8 (print)
ISBN: 979-8-9988104-3-5 (ebook)

Cover design by Maria Teressa Quiamco (@essasketch)

This is a work of fiction created solely by the author without the use of AI. Names, characters, places, and incidents either are the product of the author's imagination or are used fictitiously, and any resemblance to actual persons, living or dead, business establishments, events, or locales is entirely coincidental.

Happy birthday to my husband, who was born on Christmas Day.

And to anyone chasing the love of their life—I hope you catch them.

Playlist for Since Day One

Twice–Jake Scott

Favorite T-shirt–Jake Scott

You Don't See It–Jake Clark

Pancakes for Dinner–Lizzy McAlpine

My Home–The Change

I was Made for Loving You (feat. Ed Sheeran)–Tori Kelly

Like No One Does–Jake Scott

Glittery (feat. Troye Sivan)–Kacey Musgraves

Night Before Christmas–Sam Smith

December–Annie Tracy

Christmas is You–Elle Darlington

Lost in New York–Alex Sampson

Think I'm Gonna Love You–Michal Leah & Caleb Hearn

All I Want For Christmas Is You–Kelly Clarkson

My Gift Is You–Gwen Stefani

Take Me Home for Christmas–Dan + Shay

Lovestruck Lobotomy–VOILÀ

Since Day One

Chapter One

Bells rang out over the town square as the joyful squeals of children reached my too-cold ears. A smile pulled at my lips, and I tugged on the edges of my knitted beanie, trying to gain some semblance of warmth amidst the chill in the air. I had just shaved my face this morning, and I was mentally scolding myself for it. A beard would have kept part of my face warm. My hands were bare and cold, like my face, so I shoved them into my pockets.

I scanned the crowd while my breath clouded the air in front of me. Mom and Dad were on the other side of the snow-covered square, making hot cocoa at their annual beverage stand. A crowd of families waited in line, shifting in the cold, eager to get their warm, sugary drinks.

The wooden stand was made of worn old boards that had been painted red and white like candy canes. It was nothing extravagant, but Mom draped it in blinking white Christmas lights, making it look far happier than it did when it stood disassembled and stashed in my parents' shed the rest of the year.

It was just past seven in the evening, and the winter sun

was long gone. The sky shone bright overhead with stars that twinkled in the winter night sky, and the square was lit up like a Christmas tree. Hundreds of tiny lights surrounded the booths where customers were excitedly purchasing treats of all kinds—gingerbread, apple muffins, mini sweet-potato pies, sugar cookies shaped like snowflakes and angels.

With a deep inhale, I took it all in. The scent of pine wafted through the air, riding on the same wind as the sweet smell of spiced apple cider. The smell was tantalizing, making my mouth water.

I took a few steps in the direction of my parents, but I didn't get far before I was barreled into from behind. I grunted, turning to find my assailant. She had baby-blue eyes, long blonde hair, a red nose from the cold, and a show-stopping smile.

Her laugh drowned out the rest of the scene around me. On the daily, it drowned out the entire world, and she was often all I saw.

My smile grew.

Missouri scrambled to grab a fistful of snow from the ground. With a quick movement, I grabbed her hands, shaking the snow from them before she could shove it into my face.

"Jacob Klein, that's cheating!" Her words came out broken, lost in her laughter.

I held her hands tight, mine much larger than hers, knowing she'd attempt to pummel me with snowballs if I let her go.

"It's not cheating if I'm protecting myself from a crazy person." I matched her laugh with my own as she twisted and turned to free herself. When she finally slipped away, she'd lost both her gloves.

I made a show of holding them, my prize for winning this

round. Lifting them over my head, I turned and started back the way I was headed before I got ambushed.

My best friend ran after me. "I'm going to need those back," she said, walking calmly beside me. Her legs were shorter than mine, forcing her to rush to keep up with me.

My lips tugged up at the corner. "You can have the gloves back when you promise to play nice."

When I shifted my gaze to sneak a peek at her, she was pouting like a child.

A laugh burst out of me, and I sidestepped away from her without losing a beat in my walk. We passed my neighbors and one of our teachers from high school. We waved at them, and they waved back at both of us.

Missouri stepped closer, continuing her mission of following me.

We kept walking as our boots crunched on the snow, narrowly missing collisions with children who were amped up on candy canes and cinnamon-bun icing. Three children ran between us, almost knocking me down, and one of them lost his hat in the snow. I scooped it up and handed it back to him. He grabbed it and ran away with a *thanks* thrown over his shoulder.

"You know what happens next if you don't give me my gloves back," she said, using her sweet—yet authoritative—teacher voice, like she was talking to one of her preschool students.

I knew exactly what would happen next if I didn't give her what she wanted.

Missouri bumped my arm with her elbow. At five foot eight, she was only a few inches shorter than my five-eleven frame, something she always hated when we were kids.

After smiling at the kids passing by, she repositioned her pout.

"Oh, come on, *Misery*. You can't give me that pouty face."

Her head turned fully to face me, and when I saw her eyes, they were two glaring orbs of icy disdain. She hated that nickname, which is why I used it as often as possible.

"You know I don't like that name," she said flatly.

"Oh, I know." I shot her a wry smile, and she bit her lower lip in disgust.

I knew what was going to come next, because I always elicited the same reaction when I called her Misery. But I was still surprised by her response each time.

Maybe because I never knew how intensely she'd react. Or maybe I was always shocked by her touch, no matter what prompted it. The feeling was parallel to electrocution, like my brain was short-circuiting and I didn't know what to do with the contact, where to let the energy go so I could remain sane.

While I was distracted by my thoughts, Missouri pounced. Her gloveless fingers reached for my sides, where she knew I was the most ticklish. She was merciless, dodging side to side as I laughed and blocked her hands. Unfortunately, every time I successfully blocked one side, she lunged for the opposite. She continued giggling while I became breathless, wheezing with both laughter and my attempts to talk her away from the abuse she was inflicting on my body.

"Help!" I shouted, ready to fall to the ground.

She clapped a hand over my mouth, and her eyes became wide and serious. The tickling ceased instantly.

"What are you doing?" she said, her voice a strained whisper as she held my mouth shut.

"I'm calling for help," I said. But with her palm over my lips it sounded more like *ahm alling or elp*.

"Don't do that. Security will think there's actually something wrong and come running!" she whisper-yelled at me. Her hair fell from over her shoulders, the blonde looking lighter in the dark blue beanie she was wearing. Her thick white puffer jacket hugged her body, zipped up around her neck, and she smelled like pine trees and popcorn. "This is a huge public event. You can't just scream 'help' for no reason."

"*Ay ha a reeon,*" I replied. She removed her hand, and I repeated my statement, attempting to hide my smile. "I had a reason. I was being attacked."

I stood up a little straighter, working to smooth my coat and fix my hat that had fallen slightly askew.

Rolling her big blue eyes, Missouri held her hand out.

With a playful huff, I acquiesced to her silent demand and placed her gloves into her palm.

She closed her fingers around them and as she did, her skin slid across my palm. Missouri didn't seem to notice, or if she did, she wasn't fazed by it. I, on the other hand, felt like a hole was burning through my palm.

Without a word, she fit her thin hands into the bulky snow gloves. I rubbed my hands together to ease the burn of her touch, hoping it looked like I was fighting off the bitter cold rather than wiping away the feel of her skin from mine.

I cleared my throat. "I have to go check on my parents." I met my mom's eyes from across the last twenty feet between us. She looked delighted to see Missouri and I on our way over, and I held up my pointer finger to convey that we'd be another minute.

Mom looked over at Missouri, smiled, and gave me a contented nod.

When I turned back, Missouri continued on like the last five minutes weren't an absolute rush.

Then again, I was the only one who had feelings for their best friend, so for her it was just another day.

"Come on," she said. "I can see your mom waiting."

She linked her arm through mine, like we were a couple in

the eighteen hundreds. Only, in this modern-day scenario, we weren't.

I'd thought about it many times, what it would be like to call her mine. I'd dreamt about taking her on proper dates and kissing her under the mistletoe in this very square.

But I didn't know if she could ever return my affections at the level in which I felt them. If I ever said anything about it, it could ruin the perfect relationship we had. So I'd sworn to never announce my feelings.

I'd never tell Missouri Bellview I loved her.

It began snowing while we walked, making that cold winter night the perfect night for the town's annual Winter Extravaganza. Farmer Bob and his horse-drawn wagon passed us on the street. It wasn't a sleigh, but it did the job of toting children and parents, young couples and old, around the square. His two draft horses, Milly and Miles, were town favorites. The giant creatures were decked out in bells and had silver tinsel braided into their manes and tails. Strands of hay floated off the back of the wagon as it passed, leaving a trail on the snowy road.

Missouri smiled at the children as the wagon rolled by, and several of the younger ones waved back, shouting, "Hi, Miss Missy!" She nudged me, and I waved happily at the kids too.

"Why can't you just call me Missy like everyone else?" she asked, raising a questioning brow. "It's so much better than *Misery*." Her body shuddered at the name, which made me laugh.

I shrugged and made a show of looking at her from head to toe, then shook my head. "No. You're just not a *Missy*."

"But I am."

"Not to me."

Missy was what most of the town called her, but I never had. I'd given her an assortment of nicknames over the years

—ones that never stuck—but to me she was always just Missouri. I liked the way her name rolled off my tongue, and how every time I said it, every wonderful memory of her was wrapped up in that single word.

She thought it was weird to be named after a state. I thought it suited her.

Her parents, Brad and Susan Bellview, were in the state of Missouri on a weekend trip when her mom went into labor. They were only a few hours away from their home in Nebraska, so they ventured to drive back before going to a hospital. According to the stories, her mom arrived at our town's tiny hospital and pushed the baby out within the hour. Missouri was born, and that's how she got the name.

I looked over and met her gaze, our arms linked together as we walked in perfect unison.

When we reached the hot-cocoa stand, we walked around the table to greet my parents. They both gave Missouri big hugs, which she affectionately returned. Mom and Dad had known her since she was born, so they were like second parents to her.

I'd also known her since the day she was born, which in itself was a wild story.

We met on her first day of life because it was also *my* first day of life.

Our parents met in the hospital, both moms in labor at the same time, just one wall separating the chaos of two new lives coming into the world. When everything was done and the moms were hungry, they both sent their husbands out on a hunt for food, requesting burgers and milkshakes as well as giant iced coffees topped with whipped cream and red and green sprinkles.

It was Christmas Day.

Our dads fell into conversation at the local fast-food chain and then ran into each other once again while walking back into the hospital. They realized our families were placed in the rooms next to one another, and the rest is history. Our moms laugh about it now, how they could hear each other screaming as they labored. Missouri and I have been inseparable ever since.

"Hey, Mom," I said, wrapping her small frame in a hug. Her short brown hair was the same shade as mine, but I had my dad's height and blackish-brown eyes.

Mom looked at Missouri and asked, "Where are your mom and dad? They said they'd stop over here, but I haven't seen them yet."

Missouri pointed to the opposite corner of the square. "Their kettle-corn stand is over there by Mrs. Potter's mini trees. They've been busy too. Mom partnered with Mrs. Potter to help kids string popcorn around the tiny Christmas trees, and they get to take them home." Her eyes practically turned into hearts. "It's the cutest thing."

"Sounds like they're certainly busier than they were last year." Mom poured a cup of hot cocoa and handed it to a middle-aged woman, while Dad continued to pour for another man in line. "That's good. Your mom always has great ideas. I'm glad it's such a hit!"

Without a doubt, our moms would be sipping eggnog and chatting late into the night about the success of the festival stands this year.

I watched, folding my arms and stepping back, as the line moved along. "You've been busy yourself. The line doesn't look like it's slowed down the whole night."

Mom frowned. "We've been busy alright, but we're running out of my homemade hot-cocoa mix. I have more at the house, but your father and I don't have the time between all the customers to run back and get it."

Missouri stepped up, practically bouncing on her toes. "Jacob and I can get it, Mrs. Klein."

She looked at me for confirmation. Her left eyebrow was raised, which meant I didn't really have a say in the matter. I wouldn't say no to my mom anyway and was happy to spend the time with Missouri, no matter what we were doing.

I nodded to my mom. "Yeah, we got it. Where is it?"

"It's in the pantry, on the second shelf." Mom continued to serve the customers in line. "I put it in a red, airtight storage container."

"Here, take my truck," said Dad, handing me his keys without moving his attention away from the customers in front of him. "The snow might be too slick for your car."

I took the keys. "Okay. Thanks." I patted Dad on the shoulder as we left the hot-cocoa stand. "We should be back in fifteen minutes."

"That's fine," Mom said distractedly over her shoulder. "We'll be here."

Missouri and I walked across the snow-covered grass until we spotted my dad's red truck parked on the side of the street. Christmas music continued to ring out over the town-square speakers. Even though we were away from the hustle and bustle of the center of the square, the music and cheerful noises of the town followed us, keeping me in a jolly mood.

I rounded the truck with Missouri, opening the passenger-side door for her. She climbed in, and I grabbed her seatbelt, pulling it over her lap. Before I could click it in, our eyes met. Hers shone icy blue in the lamppost light.

She frowned in confusion, putting her hand on the seatbelt, her fingers nearly brushing mine. "Thanks," she said in a low voice, "but I got it." She took the seatbelt from my hands and buckled herself in.

I stepped back, my mind suddenly fuzzy. "Right. I was just

—watch your hands." I closed her door and walked around the back of the truck. When I was sure she couldn't see me in the side mirror, I held onto the tailgate for balance, running my other hand down my face.

Was I really going to buckle her seatbelt, like she was a child? What was I doing?

I sometimes got too caught up in Missouri—in her beauty, her joy, her excitement for life. On occasion, my heart forgot that we were just friends, and it caused me to do something stupid, like buckle her into the car.

Before she could realize I was taking too long to get in the truck, I pushed out a clarifying breath that fogged the air around me. Walking around the truck bed, I almost slipped on a slushy patch of snow but grabbed the side, regaining my balance before I completely wiped out.

When I got to the driver's door and opened it, I was met with Missouri's wide smile—the one that showed all her straight white teeth and laugh lines beside her eyes.

As always, her smile was contagious and I found myself mirroring it. "What are you laughing at?" I asked, climbing in.

"Did you just fall?"

I frowned. "What? No," I said incredulously.

She turned in her seat to face me better. "Don't lie. You fall all the time."

That was actually true; I fell all the time. I didn't have a great sense of balance, which is possibly why I preferred my desk job as an accountant. I could balance numbers, but I couldn't balance myself.

I widened my eyes at her as I pulled the truck out onto the street. "You take that back. I'm perfectly capable of walking, thank you very much."

"Maybe in your dreams," she mumbled under her breath. "Don't worry, I can give you some walking lessons."

She smirked at me, holding back another laugh, then blasted the heat through the vents and removed her boots. Her feet got cold easily, so she was always putting them on a heat source whenever she could. Tonight, it was my dad's dashboard. Her socks were white and stitched with brown teddy bears.

Without noticing my silent stare, she pulled off the hat covering her beautiful blonde hair and brushed her fingers though the tangled strands. Within the confines of the truck, the scent of her coconut shampoo mingled with the pine and popcorn I smelled on her earlier.

The drive to the house and back should have only taken fifteen minutes, but I knew without a doubt it was going to feel like a much longer car ride.

Chapter Two

We arrived at my parents' house five minutes later. It was becoming increasingly difficult for me to hide my feelings for Missouri because, putting it simply, I was just tired of hiding them. It was a constant battle to keep my romantic feelings for her separate from our regular go-with-the-flow friendship.

But if I continued pretending her every move didn't haunt me, I knew I'd go absolutely crazy.

"I'll leave the truck running," I said. "This should only take a minute. Do you want to wait here?" I kept my eyes trained on the red brick house ahead of us. It was now covered in a thin layer of freshly powdered snow.

Missouri was already opening her door.

"No, I'll come in," she said. "I want to see Purrseus."

The house sat on a mini hill with a sloping driveway. It once acted as a perfectly safe sledding hill when we were toddlers, but tonight, it was slick from the thin layer of snow. Missouri walked ahead, and I kept a few steps behind her, ready to catch her if she fell.

The roof and white porch rails were lined with twinkling

white lights, like the rest of the houses on Little Street, and the bright red front door was decked with a giant wreath Mom made herself. A big red bow hung from its side, and it was adorned with shiny gold leaves that reminded me of the golden ticket in *Willy Wonka and the Chocolate Factory*.

Stepping into the house, we were welcomed by a warm atmosphere, and the distinct smell of peppermint cookies filled the air.

"Mmm, I love your mom's peppermint cookies!" Missouri kicked off her boots, which left tiny puddles of already-melting snow on the floor in the entryway. With a hop over a few stray shoes, she bounced her way through the house, presumably in search of Purrseus.

"Misery, don't take too long!" I called after her. "We just have to find the cocoa and get back."

An annoyed—yet very cute—growl sounded from down the hall.

I snickered to myself as I walked in the opposite direction, toward the kitchen. Teasing Missouri would never get old.

The top of the kitchen cabinets stopped short of the ceiling, and Mom's favorite ornamental Christmas village rested there, where all who entered the kitchen could see it. Lights shone through the windows of the little porcelain homes, bathing the warm, deliciously scented kitchen in a relaxed state of Christmas peace.

Little pine wreaths adorned the front of the cabinet doors, and red bows rested on each one, matching the one outside. A glass jar sat on the counter filled with gingerbread men and Mom's chocolate peppermint cookies. The recipe was a family secret and a town favorite.

I grabbed one, taking a big bite and savoring the minty coolness.

When I searched the pantry, I easily spotted the container of cocoa.

"Hey," a cheerful voice said behind me.

I turned away from the pantry, cocoa mix in hand, and was met with the sight of my best friend holding Purrseus. She ran her hand over his long gray hair, and he purred loudly. He was a giant cat, but somehow he still looked like a kitten in her arms.

"He was sleeping on your bed," she said, her eyes growing wider as she looked down at the fluffy gray feline. "It was so cute."

It brought back memories of the day I got him—my twelfth birthday.

My parents had always given me two gifts, one for Christmas and one to celebrate my birthday. They felt bad that I shared my birthday with a major holiday, so they always insisted on recognizing both events as separate celebrations.

My Christmas present was a video game I had wanted for months, but my birthday present—Purrseus—was the one that topped all the gifts that year. He was tiny then. When Missouri came over that day, she cried because I got a pet and she didn't.

I told her we could share him, but that he'd have to stay at my house.

She was fine after that.

"Too bad you can't have him at your apartment," Missouri said, snuggling her face into the long fur on Purrseus's neck.

"I know. If I ever move out of my current place, I'll definitely look for a place that's cat friendly."

"At least your parents have been so nice about keeping him for you."

I chuckled. "My mom loves him. If I ever take him back,

I'm pretty sure there will be a custody battle over this little guy."

Missouri's cheeks rose up in a smile, and I reached my hand out to Purrseus, running my thumb under his chin, then my palm over his ears. Purrseus leaned his head into my hand, purring louder.

"You're such a good boy," I crooned at him.

He'd been with us for a good twelve years, and I desperately hoped we had a million more left.

Missouri rested her face against the softness of his neck once more, and I couldn't help but stare at her. The glow of the Christmas village above us illuminated the curve of her neck, the roundness of her pink cheeks, the length of her lashes. When she raised her eyes to me, my breath caught.

"Ready to go?" I asked, pushing away the not-just-friendly thoughts that kept circulating through my head.

She petted Purrseus once more, all the way down to the end of his tail, before setting him on the floor.

"You be good," she said to him. As I walked back to my boots by the front door, I heard rustling in the kitchen drawer, followed by a *pspsps*.

I rolled my eyes. She could never resist giving Purrseus treats before she left him.

A few seconds later, she appeared in the doorway with a smile.

"You're going to make him fat," I deadpanned.

She squinted her eyes at me playfully while leaning over to put on her boots. "At least he'll know he's loved, even when he's so fat he can't move."

I snickered. "He's definitely loved."

Standing, Missouri rested her hands on her hips and looked at me. "What's that look for?" she asked, an accusatory tone in her voice.

I frowned. "What look?"

"You're acting weird today."

I laughed. "Weird? How?"

We stepped outside, and I marveled at the falling snow. It was getting thicker, and I could tell we were going to be getting quite a bit overnight.

Missouri bit her lower lip as she thought, and I had to look away from her mouth to keep my thoughts of kissing her at bay. I rubbed my hands together to stave off the cold and to distract myself from the desire to touch her.

"I can't quite put my finger on it," she said, "but something's going on with you. You keep staring at me and getting a distant look on your face."

I followed her down the wet porch steps, and we slowly made our way to the truck, careful not to stumble on the slick decline. I opened the passenger door for Missouri, as I always did, but before she got in, she stopped in front of me. I had one hand on the door, keeping it from closing on us, and the other hand longed to wipe a snowflake from her cheek.

I stuck my hand in my coat pocket instead.

"I'm going to figure it out," she said. "I know something's going on with you, and I want you to tell me. I can help, whatever it is."

If only she could. My stomach was in knots at the idea of telling her my true feelings. And it only got worse the longer I waited. But I was afraid if she rejected me, I'd be crushed. We could never go back to being just friends. Our friendship would be lost forever.

I shook my head. "Nah, you can't help right now. But maybe in the future."

I guided her into the truck, and she reluctantly sat, buckling herself in before I could somehow embarrass myself again.

When I looked down at her face, she was staring at me. Snowflakes accumulated on my head and shoulders and a few tickled my nose.

"Jacob," she said softly. "Tell me what's on your mind."

"Another time," I replied, giving her a reassuring smile. "Watch your arm."

She tugged her body into the truck, and I closed her door like a gentleman.

Just as before, the ride was only five minutes from the house, but there was silence between us the entire time. The only sounds were the windshield wipers as they cleared the snow and the soft background noise of *Jingle Bells* playing over the FM radio.

Missouri uncharacteristically kept her shoes on during the ride, but I gathered it was because she didn't want to be bothered with putting them back on for the third time.

As we reached the cocoa stand, Mom looked relieved.

"Finally," she said. "What took you so long?"

I checked my watch. We couldn't have been gone for more than twenty minutes.

"Sorry, we had to drive slow because of the snow. And *Missouri*"—I stared daggers at her, feigning blame while pairing it with a cheeky smile—"just *had* to give Purrseus treats."

Mom looked at Missouri.

Missouri just smiled. "I did. It's imperative."

With a laugh, Mom took the tub of cocoa mix from my hands. "You and that cat," she said. "Whatever will he do without you around?"

I frowned, looking at Mom. "What do you mean?"

Mom stilled. She looked at Missouri—who looked horrified —then back at me, and at Missouri again.

"I'm so sorry." Her voice was a whisper, and I leaned closer to hear her. "I know you told me not to tell him yet."

"Tell me what?" *They've been keeping something from me? Something that Missouri would tell my Mom, but not* me?

Mom looked like she was about to cry while my best friend stood frozen, staring at me. The cocoa stand had a tarp covering overhead that kept the majority of the snow off us, and yet I felt the temperature dropping. The wind picked up slightly, swirling snowflakes around and between our bodies, making me aware of the space between us.

My poor, sweet mother looked between the two of us. "I'm going to give you two a minute." She ducked her head as she joined my dad, who'd been serving customers without pause. I watched as she went, and she whispered something soundless to him.

I swung my gaze back to Missouri. "What is she talking about?"

She pressed her lips together, grabbing my hand and tugging me away from the hot-cocoa stand, away from the tent covering, and away from anyone who may overhear us.

When we had gotten several feet from the noise and watchful eyes of the Winter Extravaganza, she dropped my hand. The heat and comfort of her disappeared with it.

"I was going to tell you," she started, "after Christmas. After our birthday."

We'd always said birthday in the singular sense, never birthdays as plural. Our day had always been shared, making it one big special event.

I shifted on my feet, stuffing my hands in my pockets and then taking them right back out. "Tell me what?" I could feel myself unraveling as my heart raced and my stomach twisted.

She looked down at the ground, where the snow was

slowly getting deeper, and fiddled with the collar of her jacket. "I got accepted into the master's program at NYU."

My mind raced, then stopped on those three letters. N. Y. U.

She was going to New York City.

"Wh—when?" I stammered.

She nervously pursed her lips, and she wouldn't make eye contact with me. "After New Year's. Classes start January twentieth."

I did the math in my head. January twentieth was less than six weeks away. In only five weeks, she'd be gone.

The last thing I wanted was to keep her from her dreams. I wished I could feel happy for her, but right now I was just feeling hopeless.

"Please say something," she said quietly. I scanned her eyes for any hint of… something. A look that would tell me we were going to be okay, that the distance wouldn't change a thing between us.

But instead, she just looked scared.

"Are you happy?" I asked, afraid of what I'd hear.

She nodded her head. "I'm excited I got into the program. You know I've been feeling worried about the future, about what I was going to do with the rest of my life." The ends of her hair were wet from snow, and her cheeks and nose shone red under the nearby lights strung around a pine tree. "Well, I really think this is the answer. They have a great educational leadership program, and… I think I'd be a fool to pass on it. I've also always wanted to spend time in New York, so this is kind of a two birds, one stone deal."

It made sense. Everything she said sounded right. This was the perfect opportunity for her, and I wouldn't be a good friend if I kept her from that.

"Okay." I nodded, mulling it over slowly. "I'll go with you."

"You *what*? Jacob, you can't—you have a life here."

"So do *you*," I said, hoping she could hear the sincerity in my voice.

"But you have work and your family. Think about Purrseus!"

I knew she was desperately pulling at threads when she brought the cat into the conversation. He'd always been her go-to excuse for getting me—or herself—out of situations we didn't want to be in. *We need to go home and feed Purrseus. We can't go on that family vacation in the dead of winter because who will take care of Purrseus?*

My parents had never had a problem leaving him with the neighbors for a few days, so her arguments were never found valid. Many times, it was unfortunate for both of us.

I locked my gaze on hers. "Purrseus will be fine. Look at me."

She looked at me, her eyes wide and frantic as they searched mine. I reached out and held her hand. It was cold, and I began making small circles on the back of it with my thumb.

She looked down at our fingers, at where my thumb was tracing soothing shapes on her hand, but she didn't pull away. We were used to touching each other, but not in intimate gestures like this.

"At least let me take you there, to New York," I said, filled with courage now that I was holding her hand. "Let me see where you'll be going to school, where you'll be getting your morning coffee. I want to meet your roommates—you'll have roommates, right? Are you staying on campus?"

Our eyes remained locked, and the lines on her face shifted.

She looked like she was coming to terms with the idea of me knowing and supporting her choice to go to NYU.

Her lips pulled up slightly. "Yes, I'll be staying in campus housing. It's in Brooklyn Heights." She said *Brooklyn Heights* like a queen, putting authority and decorum into her voice.

I tugged her into a hug, and she let me. I breathed her in, unwilling to ever forget her scent and how she fit perfectly between my arms. She held me around my waist, her cheek against my chest.

"I'm happy for you," I said against her wet hat. "I really am."

Her body relaxed against me. "Thank you. I'm sorry I didn't tell you sooner. I just wanted these last few weeks to be normal. Without the thought of me leaving clouding the holiday."

"I understand. It's okay."

She hugged me tighter until we both laughed, then swayed us back and forth, attempting to knock me into the snow.

We hit the ground in a heap of laughter, and we lay on our backs, allowing the snow to land on our faces. I watched as she stuck her tongue out, snatching the tiny water crystals from the air.

Snowflakes blurred my vision, but even without sight, I could describe every one of her features. I knew everything about her—how she bit her lip when she was thinking, the way her eyes creased when she laughed.

I couldn't forget the beauty of her face if I'd tried.

What would life be like without her? If she was gone, would it be too hard for me to stay? Would I travel or get another job somewhere else?

What would I do?

Everything would be different.

"We'll figure it out," she said, reading my thoughts. "The distance, I mean."

I sighed, knowing she was right. "I know."

Her timid smile permeated the deepest parts of my soul, and whatever I had planned for my life before this moment turned into a desire to do what was best for her, no matter what that looked like. Even if that meant following her to New York.

She made snow angels, and I watched, listening to her talk about NYU and how everything in the city was so different from a small town like ours. The pitch of her voice rose as she excitedly described the classes she hoped to take and the exact building she'd be housed in.

She had clearly planned the whole thing, and I was surprised she had been able to keep the secret from me this long.

However, I still had five weeks with Missouri at home.

Two weeks until Christmas and our birthday.

Right there, as we lay in the snow, I thought of what I could get her for Christmas that would top everything I'd given her before. Something special and unique. A gift that embodied everything we were to each other.

I smiled, knowing exactly what I'd get her.

Sure, I didn't have to make her fall in love with me by Christmas. But it was the most wonderful time of the year, and the magic of the holiday season could make anything possible.

If I was lucky, I'd have just enough time to win my best friend's heart before she left… And *before* the Christmas magic wore off.

Chapter Three

"Your apartment is so sad! Why don't you have a Christmas tree?" Missouri peered around my living room, spotting the empty corner by the TV and the lack of string lights over my mantel. Her face was one of pure disgust.

"I didn't think it was worth decorating this year. I'm always at my parents' house during the holiday anyway," I called back, pulling groceries out of bags in the kitchen while I watched her judge the heck out of my living space. "Their house is filled with enough Christmas cheer for all of us."

She scoffed and meandered into the open-concept kitchen. "You have to get a tree."

"Fine." I waved my hand in agreement. "I'll stop at Hobby Hub and get a little fake one for the corner."

My mind had been distracted all day by the thought of Missouri leaving Nebraska. I didn't want her to leave at all, but I also knew that if she was going, I should set up a big hoorah for all our friends to say goodbye. Mark, a buddy of mine from high school, was the first person I texted. He didn't know the depth of my feelings for Missouri, but he was a good friend to both of us, and I knew he'd help me with a party in any way he could.

He was letting all our friends know about the event, while I was planning on asking Mom to make a cake.

With an exasperated sigh, Missouri stopped directly in front of me. Her eyes were rimmed in dark eyeliner, making the blue of her irises pop, and her lashes were long and dark. She looked amazing when she wore a small amount of makeup, but I thought she looked absolutely *gorgeous* without any makeup at all.

"Jacob," she said, leveling me with a stare.

"Misery," I replied, calling her by her beloved nickname.

Her lips formed a tight line, but she didn't comment on the name. "We're getting you a tree. A real one. Today."

"Are we?" I looked into her eyes with a playful grin on my lips.

She stared back.

The distance between us could have been easily crossed, but this moment wasn't one for crossing lines. I planned to woo my best friend before Christmas, but I couldn't cross the boundary between *just friends* and *more* just yet. I couldn't risk scaring her away.

After a few seconds of us staring at one another, she frowned and stepped back. I thought I saw her blush as she tucked a stray hair behind her ear, but I couldn't be sure.

"We can go in a few minutes," she said as she looked up to meet my eyes. "Is that okay with you?"

"Of course." I continued unpacking my grocery haul, but then a thought hit me. "Hey, did you bring clothes that are warm enough for hiking through the tree farm?"

Her eyes met mine, wide and questioning. "Wait, we're going to a tree farm? I thought we'd just go to the lot and get something already cut. I mean, our families just went a few weeks ago for the parents' trees."

I shook my head at her playfully. "Oh, Missouri. Haven't you learned by now? Getting a Christmas tree is more about the experience than the tree itself." I closed the fridge after the last item was put away and rested both hands on my hips. "We've never done fake trees. It would be a scandal."

She giggled as she rolled her eyes at me. "You know I have a fake Christmas tree."

"I know," I said sardonically, rolling my eyes. "And a huge scandal that is."

She laughed at me and poked at my side.

"So," I continued, "do you have the right clothes?"

Her bottom lip stuck out. "No."

"I knew it," I sighed, pretending to be bothered by her lack of preparedness. In reality, Missouri could never bother me. "Okay, follow me."

She slipped gleefully on the wooden floor of the hallway in her fuzzy socks, following behind me as I walked to my room. I had a few clothing options she could use, albeit they'd all be a little big for her.

"You at least have a coat, right?" I asked.

"No, I don't have a—"

I stopped mid-step and turned, causing her to practically bump into my chest. She put her hands up and stepped back.

My frown was proof enough that I judged her. "You didn't wear a coat here? It's twenty-five degrees outside."

"No—I mean, I *did* wear a coat. But it's my nice one." She shrugged. "I don't want to get it dirty."

She only had two coats, insisting that having more would give her too much stress when it came to picking her outfit. Her blue coat was for playing in the snow or getting the Christmas trees when our families chopped them down together every year. Her white coat, also known as her "nice one," was used for almost everything else. She wore it anytime she was guaranteed she wouldn't get dirty.

I smirked. "You mean you came over completely unprepared to force me to get a Christmas tree today?"

"Well, yeah," she said defensively. She laughed and pushed her hand against my chest, moving me aside as she entered my bedroom. "I was under the impression that you *liked* Christmas and would already have a tree." She sat on the edge of my bed, lifting a football from the floor.

I headed straight to the closet. "You know I love Christmas. I just didn't think it was a big deal to not have a tree." I rummaged through my coats and sweaters, shifting hangers aside to find something that would work. "You'll have to roll up the sleeves, but I definitely have something you can use for today."

"Christmas is always a big deal," she said, furrowing her brows at me. "It's, like, the one holiday you absolutely can*not* skimp on." She tossed the football back and forth in her hands, then rested it on the bedside table.

I pulled out a black ski jacket with lime green and purple across the front and shoulders. It was very retro and looked like it came straight out of a '90s movie. The fabric was old, and it had a few rips on the inside lining, but it was warm and durable. It would do for today.

I held it up for her to see.

Her scrunched nose made me laugh. "This isn't a fashion show, Missouri. It's warm, trust me. You'll be happy to have it."

"Fine." She reached for the coat, but I tugged it back.

I removed it from the hanger and held it open for Missouri to put on. She gave me an odd look but turned around and stuck her arms through the sleeves. Then I put my hands on her shoulders and gently turned her back around to face me. The arms of the jacket were long, covering her hands, and it hung loosely on her straight frame.

I brought one of her hands up between us and rolled the coat sleeve up to her wrist. The rise and fall of her chest quickened, and the feel of her eyes on my face made the heat prickle across my neck. Lowering her hand, I lifted the other one just as gently, my movements slow and cautious. I relished in the feel of her body so close to mine. She didn't say anything, but her body was stiff, and I worried if I were to bump her shoulder she'd topple right over.

I rolled the sleeve up just like the first. In a moment of bravery, I allowed my thumb to lightly brush the inside of her wrist, appreciating the softness of her skin. Her fingers were long and thin, and her nails were already painted bright red for Christmas.

"Jacob?" Missouri's voice was always a comfort, but in that moment it brought me uncertainty. Was she going to push me away before I'd even confessed my true feelings?

Our eyes met, and I could feel her pulse quickening under my thumb.

"Yes, Missouri?"

Her eyes dipped to my lips, my jaw, the stubble of my beard that I hadn't shaved in a few days.

"I, um," she stammered, searching my eyes. She looked down at the carpet, our socked feet only inches apart.

Then she stepped back, and the spell was broken. Her feet left indents in the carpet where she stood, the only proof that she was ever truly standing near me at all.

Turning away, she fidgeted with the zipper on her jacket. My breath released slowly while her back was turned, and I once again needed to steady myself from the way the feel of her crashed into me, scattering my thoughts and emotions like it did every day.

"We should get going to the farm," she said, her voice cheerful and even, like she didn't just take my breath away. "I'll just use the restroom first. I'll meet you outside?"

After I gained my composure, I stepped into the hall. Missouri's jacket was zipped, and she followed behind, heading straight for the bathroom. She did everything she could to not look at me as she passed. When she shut the door, I heard the sound of water running in the sink.

"I'll start the car to get it warmed up!" I called, hoping she could hear me through the door.

The water shut off. "Okay! I'll just be a minute!"

I pulled my boots on before layering my winter coat over my hoodie. Without taking a moment to slip on my hat and gloves, I shoved them in my pocket, grabbed my keys, and welcomed the chill of December, hoping it would clear my mind and slow my racing heart.

When we arrived at Brinker's Christmas Tree Farm, we were met with a crowd of last-minute tree shoppers. I struggled to find a parking spot, but eventually got a space in the grass near the back of the lot. It was farther than I'd have liked to carry a tree, but we'd make it work.

With an excited clap of her hands, Missouri was out the door and already heading into the rows of trees.

"Wait up," I said after her. "We need to get a saw first."

She spun on her heel, blushing. "Oh, right." Her hand came up to cover her embarrassed flush, something I'd noticed her doing more of lately.

I hoped that was a good sign. A sign that maybe I made her

nervous too, in a butterflies-fluttering-in-her-stomach kind of way.

"I'm so excited!" she squealed as we got closer to the shed. The big white pom-pom on her red beanie flopped as she walked. Her hair hung loose around her shoulders, and my vintage jacket looked amazing on her. The smile she flashed at me was gold, and I filed the image away, planning to call it forward every time I missed her while she was away.

"This is the third tree we're getting this month. How can you be just as excited now as you were last time?" I asked her.

She pointed her blue-eyed gaze at me. "Because it's the happiest time of the year, Jacob!" Her laughter rang out among the trees and shoppers, earning smiles from a few of those around.

"Ho, ho, ho," I said sarcastically.

She smirked at me. "That's the spirit!"

Clearly, between the two of us, Missouri was the bigger Christmas enthusiast. I loved the holiday, and I even loved that our birthday fell on Christmas Day. But I drew the line at searching for three Christmas trees in one season.

Mr. Brinker, the farm owner, stood by a pile of saws in the shed. He had a big white beard and round glasses, and he greeted us by name like he did every time we saw him. He'd known us our entire lives. At least ever since our parents started tree shopping together when we were very young.

Missouri smiled wide and leaned in to give Mr. Brinker a hug. He looked a little taken aback, but then he smiled too, and I could tell he appreciated her show of affection.

"Weren't you just in here a few weeks ago?" he asked as she pulled away.

"We were," said Missouri, "but *someone* forgot to get a tree for his apartment." She looked over at me, and he followed her gaze.

"Well, well." He clapped me on the back. "Better late than never. Right, Jacob?"

"Right." I gave a reluctant grin, feeling like I just got reprimanded by a teacher for forgetting to do my homework.

Missouri silently laughed at me, covering her mouth with the back of her gloved hand.

"So, do you have any good trees left?" I asked Mr. Brinker.

He scratched his beard and adjusted his glasses. If he had a bigger belly, he'd pass as a perfect real-life Santa.

"Oh, lots," he said. "But it depends on what size you're looking for."

"Go big or go home, right?" I declared. "I'm thinking about seven feet?" I looked at my friend for confirmation.

She shrugged. "It's your apartment, so it's your choice. But I was just thinking something small. Like maybe four feet?"

"Four feet?" I asked incredulously. "A *baby* tree? Pass." Missouri scowled as I faced Mr. Brinker. "What do you have in the six-to-seven-foot range?"

"We have a few left, but they're not very wide. Everyone wants the full, fat ones this year, you see. You'll want to head in that direction." He pointed toward the back corner of the farm. "I think you'll find just what you're looking for."

"Thanks," I said, giving him a nod.

"Let us know if you need help hauling it out."

We waved at him and left the shed, walking through the snow in the direction he pointed.

I looked down at Missouri trotting beside me. She rubbed her hands together, and her gloves made the scratching sound of fabric on fabric.

"Do you even have enough decorations for a seven-foot tree?" she asked, reminding me of the few decorations I had tucked away in storage.

"Probably not, but I can get more."

She bit her lip, and her brows lowered.

I shifted the saw from one hand to the other. "What are you thinking about?"

She looked up at me, then back at the path we were following. "Nothing really. I was just thinking about how we've always been together, doing stuff like this. It would be weird if we weren't friends like this forever. Wouldn't it?"

She eyed the snowy pine trees as we passed. The ones near the front of the farm were short—too young for cutting, and we hiked on toward the taller trees at the back of the long rows.

"Hey, don't worry," I said. "You might be gone for a while, but we'll have each other forever. Nothing can change this." I motioned between the two of us.

What I couldn't say, though—what I kept in my heart—was that I didn't hope our friendship stayed just like this. I needed so much more from Missouri than just her friendship. I needed all of her, fully and completely.

I didn't just want her friendship. I wanted to call her *mine*.

I grabbed her hand, and she squeezed my fingers through our gloves. We walked hand in hand for a few moments, and then with three small squeezes back, I silently told her *I-love-you*.

We neared the last row of trees on the farm, and the ones we found there were massive—easily thirteen feet.

"What about that one?" Missouri joked, pointing with her free hand to the tallest one she could see.

I assessed the tree, hoping she wouldn't release my hand just yet.

"Well, I guess." I tilted my head to the side. "If we cut it into four pieces, we might be able to get it home. Think we can glue it back together in the apartment?"

She dropped my hand and swatted at my arm. "Seriously?"

I barked out a laugh. "It was your suggestion. I'm just here to make your massive Christmas tree dreams come true."

"You're impossible." She stomped off down the row of trees, and I trailed behind her.

The trees were a mix of blue spruce, Fraser fir, Monterey pine, and a few others I didn't know the names of.

We stopped at every single one. She made a comment about their sizes or coloring, and we moved on to the next. This happened about twenty times before we came to a Fraser fir reaching close to seven feet tall and perfectly shaped. It had a pointed top and was larger on the bottom while not being overly wide. There were no large gaps between the branches, giving it a full appearance on all sides.

It was the perfect Christmas tree.

"This one," I said, pointing to it with the saw.

Missouri chewed on the inside of her cheek, contemplating. She circled the tree, like a cat stalking its prey, holding her chin and tilting her head to check all the angles. She came back to me, two thumbs up in the air. "This one," she agreed. Her face beamed.

"Perfect. The sooner I get this cut, the sooner we can get out of here." I looked up at the sky as it was shifting from light blue to a shade of dark purple. "It'll be dark soon, and I think it's supposed to snow again." I crouched beside the tree and began cutting. Small branches on the underside poked at my face, and I shifted until I was lying on my side, keeping my eyes away from the pine needles and sticks.

I cut almost completely through, and as soon as the tree began to fall, I stood up.

"Watch out." I put my arm protectively in front of Missouri and watched as the tree fell to the ground.

She hugged my arm and patted my chest once. "It's perfect," she said. Then she was beside the tree, reaching down to grab it by the trunk.

I guided her back gently, handing her the saw.

"No, no," I said, unwilling to let her lift a finger. "I got this."

"I can help, you know." Her face said she wanted to help move the tree, but her posture told me she was happy to let me take over.

"I know you can," I said, "but let me do it. Besides, you can watch from behind and tell me how muscular I am." I winked at her and bent down to grab ahold of the tree's thick branches.

Missouri rolled her eyes and laughed but stepped aside with the saw as I lifted the heaviest end of the tree to drag it along the ground. As I passed her, I noticed her reddened cheeks, hoping my wink was the cause of her blush.

Chapter Four

The employees at the farm helped me lift and strap the tree to the roof of my SUV, and then Missouri asked if we could stop at the grocery store on our way to my apartment. When I asked what she needed—since we had just been there earlier—she only shrugged.

It turned out she only wanted oranges and popcorn. An odd combination of snack choices, but Missouri does what Missouri does, meaning she couldn't be contained in a box of expectations. She was a whirlwind of her own making. Pair that with my ever-growing feelings for her, and I was honestly surprised I'd survived this long as *just* a friend without getting completely swept away.

With very little help from her, we got the Christmas tree into my apartment and set it up in the corner beside the mantel and TV. Thankfully, I had a tree stand from all the past years I *did* get a tree.

Just as I finished vacuuming up loose pine needles from the carpet, Missouri walked out of the kitchen with a bowl of popcorn between her hands. The air smelled sweet, and as she got closer to me, I picked up on the scent of citrus.

"Did you eat an orange?" I asked.

She opened her palm, and I knew for certain she was peeling the citrusy fruit. "They're in the oven."

I blinked. "Did you just say you put the oranges in the oven?"

She walked past me unbothered and took a seat on the blue couch. "Yeah, to dry them out."

"For what?"

"For making garland, silly." She gave me a coy smile, then stared longingly at the bare tree in the corner.

"Have you ever made orange garland before?" I asked. It wasn't something our families had ever done, and I was curious what gave her the idea.

Wind whistled outside the dark window, rattling the glass. The snow was coming down thick and heavy.

"No, I haven't," Missouri said, "but I've always wanted to. And you needed more decorations for the bigger tree." She thumbed through her phone, hitting play on a holiday music playlist. She rested the phone on the little coffee table at the end of the couch, and the room filled with the smooth sounds of holiday notes.

Sitting beside her, I stuck my hand in the popcorn bowl to take a handful, but she pulled the bowl away before I could. "Hey, Mr. Grabby-Hands, these aren't for eating. We're stringing popcorn for the tree."

"Seriously? The oranges *and* the popcorn? You can't deny me *one* piece after you've made my whole apartment smell so delicious." I reached for the bowl again, but she held it up over her head, giving me her most serious teacher look.

Smirking, I tucked my head and barreled into her, wrapping my arms around her middle and knocking her back into a fluffy checker-patterned throw blanket. She let out a squeal of giggles as she fell onto her back.

"Jacob!" Her laughter played in my ears like the most joyful of tunes, making me weak. "You can't eat it—this popcorn is for the tree!"

With my body practically on top of hers, I reached for the bowl, but she maneuvered it around in the air, keeping it just out of reach.

"I did all the work," I managed through my laughter. "The tree doesn't deserve it. I do."

I kept reaching, and she kept dodging, her laughter close to my ear.

Suddenly, my hand bumped the edge of the plastic bowl, tipping the contents onto our heads. Missouri gasped in surprise as popcorn tumbled over her face, and I rolled off the couch, howling uncontrollably as I hit the floor. There was popcorn in her hair, falling into the V neckline of her shirt, and her mouth hung open in silent shock.

Leaning forward on my knees, I grabbed a piece of popcorn from her shoulder and ate it.

"You had to make that so difficult." I chewed the popcorn, smiling while I eyed all the food on the couch and floor.

Missouri's face melded seamlessly from a scowl to a wide, amused grin, and then she laughed her most genuine laugh. I watched in awe as I contemplated how I got to be so lucky.

She ate a few pieces from the couch. "I hope you know I'm not cleaning all this up. This is your fault." She raised a brow, pointing to me with a handful of popcorn.

I spotted another piece in her hair, just behind her ear. I leaned forward, reaching for it, and I swore I saw her lean toward my hand. Something electric passed between us, and I wondered if this was my chance. The moment I revealed my true feelings.

With hesitant fingers, I removed the popcorn from her hair. Then, just to see how she'd respond, I smoothed her hair down with the palm of my hand. She froze, her eyes on mine, and I couldn't decipher the meaning of her stillness.

Was she still because she was waiting for more? Or was she frozen in shock, planning her quickest route out of here?

"Is this... okay?" I asked in a hushed tone.

Her eyes remained focused on mine, and she nodded slowly as I ran my fingers through her smooth golden hair. Her eyes closed, and she shivered under my touch.

"Jacob?" The comforting way she said my name was gone. This time, it was unsure and timid.

"Yes, Missouri?"

"We should..." She stopped and opened her eyes. "We should bake cookies!" She jumped from the couch like it burned her, then pulled her hair back, tying it into a low ponytail.

I watched from the floor, unable to stand. "Uh, sure." I rubbed at the back of my neck, processing that I came so close to kissing her. "What about the popcorn?" I asked.

"We can do it later. Or, maybe I should just go. Should I go? The snow is getting bad out there." Her words were clipped, and her movements were rigid. She walked to the window, peering out at the snow accumulating on the street.

"No," I replied, my voice rushing out a little too quickly.

She turned from the window to face me.

"Don't go home just yet," I said, giving her a pleading look. I knew my eyes gave away my desperation, but I wasn't ready for our evening to be over.

She pressed her lips together. "What if the weather gets too bad to drive home later?"

I wiped a nervous palm down the side of my sweatpants. "Then I'll drive you back in my SUV or you can stay the night here. It wouldn't be the first time we've had a sleepover. I'll stay on the couch." I gestured toward the navy couch, now covered in popcorn, with the throw blanket halfway on the floor.

"Are you sure?"

"Totally sure," I said, managing to keep my voice steady as I got up from the floor.

The problem was, I wasn't totally sure this was a good idea at all.

"Well... okay then. I'll start getting the ingredients out for cookies." She passed me on her way to the kitchen, and for a second, our eyes met. There was a look on her face I'd never seen before, something new and exciting in the way her eyes sparkled back at me.

My stomach lifted with the weightless feeling of hope. A dangerous thing for a man to feel.

"Chocolate chip or sugar cookies?" Missouri asked me from the kitchen.

I liked chocolate chip cookies the best, but I knew they weren't her favorite.

"Sugar cookies," I said, following her into the kitchen. "But are you sure we shouldn't finish the popcorn garland first? You also have the oven filled with oranges right now."

I pointed at the oven, and she stared.

Then her brows creased, like she was remembering what she was looking at. "Oh. I forgot." Her shoulders fell in disappointment.

The scent of the oranges was beginning to spread throughout the apartment, getting stronger as the fruit cooked and dried.

"How long do they have to be in there?" I asked, nodding my chin toward the oven.

"A few hours." She crunched her nose, and leaned her elbows on the kitchen island. "It's fine. We have plenty of time before Christmas to practice my cookie-baking skills."

"Cookie-baking skills?" I leaned on the counter across from her. "Is that a skill you planned to correct—I mean, *perfect*—this year?"

"I'm not that bad."

I raised a brow.

"Okay, I'm pretty bad." She laughed at herself. "But I wanted to surprise your mom with a really good batch this year."

"I think your cookies are always fine." I shrugged.

Missouri stared at me as if I just grew a third eyeball.

"What?" I said, raising my hands in defense. Knowing Missouri, she would jump over the counter and tackle me if she thought I was making fun of her.

Her hands moved to her hips. "Don't try to act like my cookies have ever been good. I know they're not. Especially compared to your mom's cookies."

I waved toward the living room, and she followed me.

I smiled encouragingly at her. "Seriously, I think your cookies have always been good. I eat them every year."

She picked up a roll of thread I hadn't seen on the coffee table earlier, then leveled her eyes at me. "You're the only one who ever eats the cookies I make."

That's true. Her cookies weren't the best, but they were special because she made them.

I just shrugged again. "You shouldn't mess with a good thing. I'll eat them no matter what they taste like."

"Right," she said, her eyes growing thoughtful as she stared at me. "You shouldn't mess with a good thing."

Her voice trailed off, and I scooped up the remaining mess of popcorn while Missouri got to work threading a needle. She began piercing kernels with the needle, threading them onto the long thread laid across her lap.

"So tell me more about NYU," I said, sitting on the couch

beside her. I left space between us so she could work, and so I could breathe despite the way my heart beat harder when she was near.

"Are you sure you want to hear about it?" She gave me a sideways glance.

"Yeah. Why wouldn't I?" I responded.

"Because I know you're upset that I'm leaving." She lowered her eyes from mine, focusing them instead on the popcorn.

"Nah," I say, pushing a heavy amount of casualness into my tone. "I'm happy for you."

Her lips pulled up into a half smile. "Are you really?"

I sat back against the couch, stretching my arms out along the top. "Of course I am. Are you still okay with me coming to New York to drop you off?"

"Yes!" She almost knocked the popcorn bowl back onto the floor in her excitement, but she recovered quickly and gave me an apologetic smile. "I mean, I didn't know if you would still want to do that after you had some time to think about it. New York is so far to travel to just drop me off at school."

I threw a piece of popcorn in the air and caught it in my mouth. "We can make a vacation out of it. Go ice skating at Rockefeller Center, see the giant tree, tour campus."

Her eyes lit up.

"It would be fun," I said.

"I've always wanted to do those things, but I thought I'd have to do them alone." Our gazes connected, and her smile felt warm with the view of the snowfall in the window behind her. "Thank you, Jacob. It'll be the best New Year ever."

She was right. It would be the best New Year ever because I planned to kiss her from the last day of December into the first day of January and every day after that if she'd let me.

Chapter Five

Missouri and I stepped back to observe our work. Wrapped in tiny white lights that cast shadows on the walls and sporting a garland of oranges and popcorn that draped in layers across its branches, the tree was finally complete.

I surprised myself by actually liking the way it looked. It wasn't what I was used to seeing on my trees, but it was refreshing and bright. Just like Missouri.

"It looks great," I told her, wrapping an arm around her shoulder.

She leaned into me, gazing contentedly at the tree we spent hours decorating.

"Yeah," she agreed, "it looks perfect." She yawned.

"Alright, let's get you to bed, sleepy-head. I've already changed the bedsheets for you, and there's an extra toothbrush in the drawer by the bathroom sink. You can look through my drawers to find something to sleep in, if you want." I tidied up around the couch, laying a pillow and blankets over it for myself. "Do you need anything else?"

"Nope," she said. "Thanks for letting me stay here."

Decorating the tree took much longer than we expected. Missouri realized she had to bake the orange slices for a whole three hours to properly dehydrate them. The snow had been falling steadily since we were at the tree farm, and we both agreed it wasn't safe for us to drive on the slippery roads, especially late at night.

"You know you're always welcome here." I held my arms open, and she dipped into my embrace. She hugged my waist, and I left a soft kiss on her hair, so featherlight she may not have noticed it.

"Good night," she said, pulling away.

I let her go and watched as she walked quietly down the hall to my room.

When I woke, it was to the sound of swooshing, like socks gliding across the floor, and the thump of a cabinet door closing. I covered my eyes, guarding them against the harsh light from the window.

I sniffed the air. It still smelled like oranges and popcorn, mingled with the scent of pine. But there was another scent in the air, one that made my stomach growl from hunger.

Throwing the blankets off, I padded from the living room to the kitchen.

Missouri was standing at the stove with her back to me, swaying her hips as she mixed something in a large bowl. Her long blonde hair was out, wavy and untamed from a night of sleep. She was wearing a T-shirt and sweatpants—both mine— and on her head were my large white headphones.

She hadn't noticed me, and I leaned on the doorframe to

watch as she danced silently in my kitchen. My clothes were too big on her, and her hair was a mess, but I could look at this perfectly raw version of her every morning forever and be completely happy.

Her socks slid on the wooden floor, her shoulders bounced, and as she spun, her eyes met mine. She froze and pulled the headphones from her head.

"Hey," she said, looking more self-conscious than ever.

I pushed off the doorframe, smiling sleepily. "Good morning. What are you making?"

"Pancakes. You had some kind of protein pancake mix in your pantry, but I added a few things to spice it up."

I lifted a quizzical brow and sat at the kitchen counter. "Is that your way of saying you added a bunch of sugar?"

She scoffed. "No, it means I added a *little* bit of sugar, some cinnamon, and a dash of nutmeg." She turned back to the pancake on the stove. With smooth movements, she flipped the pancake onto a plate and placed it in front of me.

"Thanks," I said. "It smells great."

"I hope it tastes great too," she responded. "I may be terrible at baking cookies, but I can make a mean pancake."

There was a bottle of syrup on the counter, so I added a little to my pancake and scooped a large bite into my mouth. I was transported to pancake heaven.

"Mmm," I hummed, gesturing toward my plate. "This is amazing, Missouri. Seriously, it tastes like Christmas in my mouth." I took another big bite, savoring the cinnamon flavor and the fluffy texture. "Why did I not know you could make great pancakes?"

She laughed, looking genuinely flattered by my compliment, and turned back to the batter, pouring more onto the pan. It sizzled, and I saw that she'd already been eating while she cooked—there was a plate beside the stove with half a pancake, covered in a little too much syrup, whipped cream, and red sprinkles.

"Wait," I said, "why didn't I get offered sprinkles?"

Laying the spatula down, she turned back to me. "Because you don't like sprinkles."

"Yes, I do."

She rolled her eyes. "That's not true."

"How do you know everything about me?" I laughed.

"Because..." She narrowed her eyes playfully at me. "It's my job to know everything about you. If I didn't, I'd be the worst best friend ever." She turned back to flip the pancake on the pan.

I thought it funny that she knew almost everything about me when she didn't know the most important secret I'd kept for the past twelve years.

I walked around the counter, sprayed a normal amount of whipped cream on my pancake, and sat back down.

"Oh," I continued, "my mom texted me last night. Your parents are going over to their house this morning for coffee, and they want us to come for a gingerbread-house competition at noon."

A groan escaped her throat. "Nooo, not again."

I pressed a hand to my chest. "Wait. Hold on. Is there actually something about Christmas that Missouri doesn't like?" I bit back a smile.

She turned the stove off and brought her plate to the counter. "I don't mind making gingerbread houses, but you remember how last year went. My dad was way too competitive. He made the whole thing *not* fun."

"Isn't that the point of a competition—to be competitive?" I joked, trying to lighten the mood. But when she mentioned it, I remembered the fiasco that was last year's gingerbread-house competition. Missouri's dad rushed her and didn't take her ideas into account. He even said that if they didn't win, there was no point in doing a competition at all.

Her eyes created slits as she stared at me over the counter. "Yes, a little friendly competition is fine. But I *cannot* get paired with my dad again."

Her dad was the football coach for our town's high school, so everything he did was in the spirit of competition.

After Missouri and her dad were paired together for the gingerbread-house competition, she spoke to me about little else over the next week other than how her dad made her feel like he was just coaching one of his athletes rather than having fun with his daughter.

"Just promise me you'll be my partner," she said, her eyes desperate.

I leaned back and crossed my arms. "Of course I will. You have nothing to worry about."

A few hours later, I pulled up to my parents' house in my SUV. I waved at Missouri as she parked behind me and met her at her door.

"Did your tires slip on the way over?" I asked her as she got out.

"Not much. I'm just glad the plow trucks have already been over all these roads."

The snow was easily a foot high after last night's snowstorm, but the driveway and porch steps were already shoveled clear. When we reached the front door that held Mom's homemade wreath, we were greeted by the sound of jolly

Christmas music ringing through the walls. We stepped inside, stomping the snow off our boots as we did.

Mom came running from the kitchen, little silver bells on her red sweater jingling all the way.

"They're here!" she shouted down the hall.

"Hi, Mom," I said, leaning down to hug her.

Mom hugged Missouri, then turned down the hall to where I assumed the rest of the parents were.

"Phil, Jacob's here!"

Dad appeared, ambling toward us, with Brad and Susan Bellview following behind. They were all wearing Christmas sweaters in varying shades of red and green, each one arrayed with little bells that rang as they moved. A cacophony of "hellos" sounded in the entryway. I got a pat on the shoulder from Missouri's dad, and then her mom appeared at my side, giving me a tight squeeze. She was an identical reflection of her daughter, with long blonde hair and light blue eyes.

"Oh, I almost forgot," said Mom. "We got you both Christmas sweaters too."

I met Missouri's eyes, and from the face she made at me, mine were likely shining with the same portrayal of emotions as hers—amused, embarrassed, and a little worried.

"I forgot you still do the sweater thing," Missouri mumbled to me under her breath.

Mom caught it. "Of course we do. It's a tradition I don't plan on ever stopping." She opened the small closet in the hallway and retrieved two plastic bags, which she held out to us. "Here."

I held the bag open and peeked inside. It was a green sweater with bells sewn on in obnoxious clumps. I watched Missouri. She looked just as excited as me to be matching our parents.

Despite the fact that both of us were turning twenty-four in less than two weeks, our parents found joy in forcing us to follow the traditions they created when we were children.

"What color is yours?" Missouri asked me, her disinterest written plainly across her blank face as she cocked her head to the side.

"Green. Yours?"

"Same."

Everyone remained in the entryway, carefully watching us.

"Well?" Mom urged. "Go change, and then we can start the competition."

Our dads headed back to the living room where a loud football game played on the TV while my mom led Mrs. Bellview into the kitchen. They whispered like schoolgirls and then burst into laughter when they were finally out of eyesight.

"I guess we're actually doing this," I said, pulling my sweater out of the plastic bag.

Missouri filled her cheeks with air, then blew it out slowly before walking into the hallway bathroom. "I guess we're still doing this," she said with a defeated tone and closed the door.

When I met her in the hall two minutes later, she looked annoyed. Her cheeks were red, and she pulled at the rounded neckline of her sweater. When the bells rang from the movement, her scowl deepened.

"Why the long face?" I said, stopping in front of her. I kept my voice low so the parents couldn't overhear us.

"I just don't like having to wear this," she replied. "It makes me itchy."

A rash had already begun forming on her neck, a sign that she was stressing out.

"Hey, stop scratching it." I took her hands in mine and moved them away from her neck. "What's wrong? And don't tell me it's the sweater."

She lowered her eyes to the floor, then up and down the hall before taking a step closer to me. "I'm freaking out about how my dad is going to act." Her voice was so low I strained to hear it.

"It'll be fine. I already told you I'll make sure Mom puts you and me together."

"I know, but…" Her eyes shifted down the hall again. "He'll be hypercompetitive with anyone. It's embarrassing."

"I think it will be okay." I leveled my eyes with hers. "But if you want to leave, I'll go with you. If this is all too much, we don't have to stay. Just say the word."

The inside of her lip was probably going to bleed with how much she was chewing on it. She shifted on her feet, thinking it over.

"No." She shook her head. "I can stay."

"Are you sure? You know I'll go if you want to."

Her lips formed a tight smile, and she nodded. "I don't want to leave my mom and your parents."

"Okay," I whispered, dropping her hands. "Let's go then."

I put my arm over her shoulders and guided her into the kitchen. Mom called the men in as soon as she saw us, and when we were all gathered around the counter, she clapped her hands, an excited smile spreading across her face.

Missouri smiled too, her face softening around my mom's excitement.

"Everyone come into the dining room," Mom said, ushering us toward the scent of cookies and sweets. We walked through the kitchen to the dining room, everyone's Christmas sweaters jingling along to the music that played over the speakers.

The dinner table was covered in a plastic holiday-themed tablecloth. There were three spots set up as work stations and at least fifteen bowls of candies and other edible decorating materials in the middle. The chairs were each paired into sets of two, and we each took a seat.

"Alright. Let's get started," said Mom, standing at the head of the table. "The rules are simple. When one hour is complete, we all stop what we're doing, and the team with the best-looking house is the winner. Missy and Jacob are team number one this year, Brad and Susan—team two, and Phil and I are team three."

"Got it. What's the prize?" Mr. Bellview asked, rolling up the sleeves of his red Christmas sweater.

Missouri stiffened beside me. She was a fan of fun, but she'd never been easygoing in a scene doused in competition.

I placed a hand lightly on the middle of her back, letting her know I was here. I felt her body relax under my touch, and she smiled gratefully at me.

"The winning team doesn't have to do any clean up on Christmas Day," Mom said. Everyone's eyes lit up, imagining a relaxing holiday with no clean-up duties.

"Ready?" I asked Missouri.

"Ready."

Mom started the timer, yelling "GO," and everyone grabbed at the pieces of gingerbread laid out before them.

With my hands full of delicious gingerbread walls, Missouri squeezed the piping bag to layer the icing along the edges of the cookies. It took a few minutes and several attempts, but once we had the walls up, we joined the roof together like a tent. Once the structure was sound, she started drawing windows and a door with the white icing.

Hands were everywhere. Gumdrops fell on the ground, and peppermint rounds rolled across the table. A bowl of sprinkles got tipped over in the rush, and our moms both screamed and giggled like little girls.

Missouri and I made eye contact, silently rolling our eyes.

Neither of us had siblings, but I imagined what we had was equivalent to sibling telepathy.

From the other end of the table, I could see Mr. Bellview frowning while he meticulously placed red licorice candy along the roof of their house. Mrs. Bellview stuck green M&M's into icing along the lower edge of the house to act as grass, but her husband made a quiet remark and removed them, replacing them with green sprinkles instead. She ignored whatever he said, moving on to put more icing on the roof that resembled snow.

When I looked over at Missouri, she was watching her dad. He was oblivious to the attention.

Her fingers balled into a fist on the table, and I rested my hand over hers, tugging it under the table and onto my lap. I gave it three gentle squeezes. When she looked at me, her lips tugged into a half smile, and we continued working on our gingerbread house. It was obvious Missouri tried to ignore her dad during the competition phase of the afternoon, and I tried my best to keep her busy and distracted so she wouldn't be tempted to keep her eye on him.

We all spoke to one another over the sound of Christmas music in the background, and the tempo of the songs kept us moving at a steady pace. Mom and Dad's house leaned a little to the side, and there was a lot of excited shouting as they raced the clock to fix their mistakes.

At the end of the hour, we all put our hands up and stepped back from the table like we were on a TV bake-off show.

Scanning the table, we eyed one another's houses, silently hoping our house was the best one standing.

"And that's the timer," Mom says. "Brad, you can't touch it anymore." She frowned, waving her hand at Missouri's dad, who was trying to add one more green M&M to his house.

Funnily enough, he was putting the M&M's where his wife was placing them earlier before he told her not to.

"Does that disqualify them?" asked Dad, laughing jokingly.

"No. But it should, since you were cheating." She eyed the Bellviews, then looked toward me and Missouri. When she saw our gingerbread house, she threw her hands up in defeat. "Honestly, it's not even a competition. Just *look* at Jacob and Missy's house. It's immaculate for being made of gingerbread cookies."

All eyes turned to us and the colorful candy home we created.

"Yup, that's a winner right there." Dad's voice sounded pleased as he stood. He enjoyed the family traditions, but this was one he was always happy to be done with when it ended.

"Aww, it's so cute," trilled Mrs. Bellview. "You two did an amazing job." She walked around the table to get a better look, and Mom joined her.

The men shook hands. Mom and Dad's dilapidated house fell over, making the moms laugh some more, and we all picked at the leftover candy strewn across the table as we cleaned up the mess.

"You did great building those walls," Missouri said to me, handing me a bag for the leftover red licorice.

"It was a team effort," I replied.

She watched as our parents carried supplies back to the kitchen, then leaned in close. "Thank you for teaming with me so I wasn't with my dad."

I nodded, meeting her eyes. "Of course. Anything for you —you know that."

Her soft smile grew, and she looked away quickly as her mom came in to wipe down the table.

I gazed around the room, and soaked it all in—the way our

families fit together, the team Missouri and I made. My mind wandered, thinking of all the future Christmases we'd have. Would we still be friends the way we are now, or would I be able to call her something more?

And if she didn't ever fall for me the way I'd fallen for her, would our friendship and all our future Christmases be lost?

Chapter Six

Monday morning was another cold day, biting and bone-chilling like all the days of December. However, the sun was still shining brightly, and I couldn't help checking the time every five minutes. I leaned my elbows on my work desk, trying to get a couple more hours of work completed before lunch. It was difficult. I felt my time with Missouri slipping away through my fingers. I hated that we both had work —this thing that was stealing our precious time together and keeping us apart.

Nonetheless, I planned to pick up Missouri's favorite hot coffee during my lunch break and bring it to her at the school. She usually needed to eat with her preschoolers, but we could sometimes meet for a few minutes if I brought her lunch. Today I had to rush back for a meeting with a client, but I couldn't *not* see her. Her hold on me had only gotten stronger over the past few days.

The time ticked by slowly as papers covered my desk, the stack feeling endless. I checked my watch, hoping it would tell me I could finally leave to see my best friend. As soon as I saw the time, I jumped to my feet, and with one quick click, I locked my desktop screen and grabbed my wallet and keys.

After stopping at a coffee shop that Missouri frequented, I drove straight to the preschool. I parked and pulled out my phone, typing a quick message. *Come outside. I have a treat for you.*

Not two minutes later, she crossed the parking lot, arms wrapped around her middle, her long white coat bundled around her body. She was wearing flats that showed the tops of her feet, making me feel colder just by looking at her. I got out of the car and met her in the middle of the parking lot.

"I didn't know you were coming today," she said, smiling as she stepped over small mounds of snow.

"I wanted to surprise you." I handed her the steaming cup of coffee.

Her eyes widened in surprise. "You went to Sammy Joe's for me?"

"Well, yeah. I know it's your favorite." I stood with my hands in my pockets, wishing we had more time together.

Her smile reached her eyes as she took a tentative sip from the cup. "It's *so* good. Thank you." She looked at my car. "Did you get yourself one?"

"No, but I got a smoothie and a sandwich for lunch." I nodded toward my car, which was still running. "Actually, I have to get back to work for a meeting, but... I wanted to see you."

Her head tilted to the side as she took me in, and then a small smile tugged at her lips. "I wanted to see you too."

A tumbling feeling started in my chest, and it rushed all the way to my feet. We had inside jokes and were always teasing each other, but we'd never flirted. I always held that part of myself back.

But in just a few days, all that had changed. Now I wanted nothing more than to flirt with my best friend.

I couldn't help but think that maybe we were finally crossing that bridge together. The one I'd already been crossing over the past twelve years. In my mind, I'd been holding my hand out to her, waiting for her to make the choice to follow.

My blood pumped faster thinking she might finally be grabbing hold.

I stared back at her, my lips in a frozen smile. I was in a trance. I couldn't move. Going back to work was the last thing I wanted to do.

She laughed lightly, pulling me from my stupor.

"Can we have lunch together tomorrow?" I asked, hoping she could get away from the children for just a few minutes.

The afternoon sun shone down on the slightly wet pavement, lighting up her eyes. "I'll ask Breanna if she'd be okay with the kids on her own during lunch. I'll text you to let you know what she says."

"Perfect."

"I have to get back inside," she said. "My feet are absolutely freezing, and I have a heater in my room that I like to put my feet by. It's calling my name."

"Yeah," I said, smiling at the very Missouri-like statement. "Yeah, of course."

"Thanks for the coffee."

"Anything for you." I paused.

She was fighting a smile, turning her body away as she did.

My core heated, and I turned to my car as she walked back toward the school entrance.

"One more day?" I shouted across the parking lot.

She turned abruptly, smiling wide. She was beautiful.

"One more day!" she shouted back.

One more day of teaching before she was off for the Christmas break. It was also her last day teaching before she left for New York.

My mind spun with all the holiday fun I had planned for us.

The next day, I'd planned a perfectly delicious lunch for the two of us. I didn't have any meetings, and I'd asked my boss if I could have an extra thirty minutes for lunch. He said as long as I made it up sometime during the week, he didn't see a problem with it.

Just like yesterday, I drove into the school parking lot and texted Missouri.

She walked out the door, her smile growing when she spotted me. I walked around the car and opened the passenger door for her.

"Are we going somewhere?" she asked, the question shining in her eyes.

"Nope." I popped the p and closed the door for her once she got in. Then I walked back around and got in on the driver's side.

"Something smells good in here." Missouri tilted her head back, sniffing the air as she removed her coat.

I reached into the back seat, and as I did, I got a whiff of her scent: coconut and something else. Paint?

"Were you painting?" I asked, bringing a large brown paper bag into the front seat.

"Yeah, my class was doing a little project for their parents for Christmas."

I opened the bag and started pulling out boxed tacos and

small containers of salsa, guac, and sour cream. "What was the project?"

"What—" Her voice trailed off, and when I looked at Missouri, her eyes were wide with disbelief, staring at the items I kept pulling out of the bag.

A satisfied smile worked its way onto my face. "I asked, what was the project? For the parents."

She shook her head, and chuckled. "Oh, right. The kids had to paint a mini paper plate and decorate it as a Christmas tree ornament. You know, the little paper plates that are used for cake at parties?" As she talked, she removed her boots. They were brown with a little heel, and they came up to her ankles. They looked nice on her, paired with jeans and a red knit sweater that she wore for her last day of teaching. When the boots were off, she put her feet up on the dashboard, close to the vents.

"Sounds cute." I grinned.

"They were adorable." She eyed the food, which I'd been gingerly placing on the center console between us, doing my best to balance it all. "Okay, enough talking," she said. "I need to eat this. My mouth is literally filling up with saliva."

A laugh rolled out of me because I was also salivating, the scent of the tacos filling my car with spicy goodness. "Take what you want; it's all for you."

She looked up at me skeptically. "It can't be. Did you already eat?"

"No. I didn't. But I got a bunch of everything and wanted you to pick what you like first." I rubbed at a spot on my chest with my fingers. "I actually forgot what you order at Dos Amigos, so that's why I got... everything."

"That's really sweet of you." Her blonde hair was pulled over one shoulder, braided loosely, and her eyelids were a little shimmery from her makeup. The pink of her cheeks looked like it could have been from more than just the cold, maybe makeup as well. Or maybe my romantic gestures of bringing her favorite things to her workplace were paying off, making her feel things for me she hadn't felt before.

"It was nice of Breanna to watch the kids so you could eat with me," I said, remembering she had to make plans with her assistant teacher before she could agree to lunch.

"She's always really helpful, especially when you're involved." She raised her eyebrows, laughing. "I told her my friend Jacob wanted to have lunch with me, and she practically threw me out of the building."

The corner of my lips tugged upward. "I remember Breanna. She's cool."

"She remembers you too," she said, smirking at me. "She was at the Christmas Extravaganza, and she said she saw you at my side the entire night. Said you were the sweetest golden retriever she's ever seen."

A laugh bellowed out of me because that was actually a pretty accurate picture of me when it came to being at Missouri's side.

"I love that girl," I said through my laughter. Missouri eyed me, and something inside me flipped at the thought of her being jealous. "What? She's happily married. You know I don't mean it like that."

She hummed her understanding and continued eating her taco.

I didn't tell her that I had my eye on someone else. Someone who'd already had my heart for a very, very long time.

"So, last day," I said, grabbing a burrito when she pushed it toward me. I started unwrapping it from the foil, and Missouri twisted the cap open on a fizzy drink.

She took a long sip, then answered, "I'm so ready to be

done with the semester, but I'm going to miss teaching when I go to New York." She leaned her head on the headrest and looked at me, her eyes cloudy.

I sat up, frowning. "Hey, it's okay. What's wrong?"

She frowned and laid her food on the foil resting in her lap. "I thought I really wanted to go to NYU. I thought I wanted to get my master's and become a principal. But, Jacob, I love the kids. I love the classroom and seeing their little faces light up." She shook her head, her braid swaying against her shoulder. "I'm not sure if I want to be behind a desk all the time."

She held up her hands, showing me splotches of paint that I assumed didn't wash off when she tried. "I want to get paint on my hands and be the one in the classroom teaching. What if I'm not the right kind of person to be a principal? What if I hate it?"

I pressed my lips together. If she decided to stay home and forgo the offer at NYU, then half my problem would be solved. She wouldn't be leaving, but I'd still be in the friend zone.

I mentally crossed off that option, kicking it where the sun didn't shine. There was no way I'd be staying in the friend zone past Christmas.

"You haven't gone to New York yet, so it's technically not too late to change your mind about going." I wouldn't tell her not to go, knowing she needed to make this decision for herself.

She bit into her chicken taco, speaking around it as she chewed. "That's true. But what if I don't go, and that's the wrong choice?" She swallowed. "What if I keep teaching here in January, but then next fall I'm wanting to get my master's again and I've already lost my spot at NYU?" Her palms came up to her forehead, and she laid her head back on the headrest once more.

She let out an exasperated sigh, a sound that I made often

when I was alone. I could relate to the frustration of being stuck between two paths, unsure if taking either one would land me in the position I could only dream of.

"Listen." I set my food down and turned my body as much toward her as I could in the front seat. "I don't have the answer for you, and I'm not going to tell you what you should do. But I think if you're scared of missing out on this opportunity, then you should go for it. And on the other hand, if you're completely happy doing what you're already doing, you should stay here."

Silence filled the space, and then she exhaled, raising a brow at me. "Jacob, was that supposed to be helpful?"

I took another bite of my burrito and rolled my eyes. "Sorry," I said between bites. "I'm not exactly jolly St. Nick with a bag full of good cheer."

She laughed, then grabbed her drink and took a sip. "No," she said, "you're certainly not qualified for that job title."

We continued eating, recalling how relatively well the gingerbread competition went two days ago.

"At least my dad didn't act out when my parents lost," she commented.

"I know it really bothers you when your dad is in competition mode, but he's really not that bad at any other time."

"I totally agree with you." She started pulling on her boots and zipping them up in the back, a sign our time together was coming to an end. "I have five more minutes," she said, noticing me watching her.

When her boots were on, she pulled on her coat and sat back. "My dad didn't use to be so competitive. It only started when he began coaching full time. It's like he can't shut it off. And I know it's only worse because it's football season. He's under a lot of pressure." Her shoulders moved up and down in a small shrug. "It's the one thing I don't like about the holidays. My dad's stress turns into my stress, and I don't want to put that on anyone else. It has to stop on me, but I don't know what to do with it."

I hadn't realized how much her dad's work stress played into her life and affected her. She was always so positive and joyful—she didn't let anything get her down.

Except this apparently.

I hated that I didn't notice how big of a deal it was for her. That it wasn't just the yearly gingerbread competition, but other times as well.

"I thought it was just the gingerbread-house competition that bothered you," I said slowly. "Why didn't you tell me about this before? That you were feeling stressed because of your dad during the holidays?"

She met my eyes. "Because I didn't want you to think badly of him. He adores you, and I know you've always looked up to him." Her gaze dropped from mine.

"Don't do that," I said.

Her frown deepened as her eyes shot back to me. "Do what?"

"Keep things from me. I can handle it. Whatever's bothering you, anything you need to talk about, tell me. You know I'm always here for you."

She gave me a tight smile. "I know. Thanks." Stuffing the last bite of her taco into her mouth, she mumbled, "That goes for you too. You still haven't told me why you were acting weird at the Extravaganza."

Her mouth was so full, I could hardly understand what she said.

"You know taco is spelled T-A-C-O, not T-A-L-K-O, right?" I joked, turning the subject away from me before she dug deeper.

She shoved my arm and opened the door, letting in the

bitter cold air. When she was out of the car, she stuck her head back in. "So you want to hang out tomorrow, right?"

"I have work."

She frowned and scrunched up her nose. "Gross."

I raised my brows and felt the corner of my lips twist up. "Just because you get off for the holiday, doesn't mean the rest of the working class get to do the same."

"Then just do what I'm apparently doing." She winked at me. "Quit." She pushed the door shut and walked across the parking lot.

I watched her as she went, loose hairs from her braid billowing behind her in the slight breeze. Just before she went into the school, she turned back and waved.

A smile stretched across my face. If only she knew just how quickly I'd quit my job and follow her to New York if she asked.

Chapter Seven

Wednesday and Thursday proved to be long days at the office, and I found myself checking my watch frequently until the clock hand finally hit five. Each day, I bolted home to shower and change, excited to spend the evenings with Missouri. She had been experimenting with her cookies, trying to make the perfect ones to bring to my parents' house on Christmas Day.

Every year, Missouri and I celebrated our birthday on Christmas Day, splitting the day in half. The morning hours were for Christmas—breakfast, gifts, a light lunch made up of sugar cookies and Mom's assortment of pastry goods—while the rest of the day was designated to our birthday celebration. Our parents spent a lot of the time with us, regaling us with many embarrassing stories of us in diapers, but it was always a good time.

On Friday, I'd just logged out of my desktop when my phone rang. It was Missouri.

The corner of my lips pulled up.

"Hi," I said, answering the call. "I'm just about to leave work."

We'd spent every day of the past week together, which wasn't unusual for us. But hearing her voice made my body feel electric, like fireworks were exploding in my stomach.

I chased that feeling.

"I just can't do it, Jacob. It's not going to work out." Missouri's voice came through the phone in quick, almost panicked irritation.

"Hold on. Back up. You can't do what? What won't work out?"

If she was talking about New York, then that meant she was really thinking of staying here in Nebraska. My mind raced at the thought and all the possibilities.

"The *cookies*," she breathed out.

My stomach dropped.

"They're all coming out wrong," she continued. "Your mom's going to hate them."

Holding the phone between my ear and shoulder, I packed up my work bag, grabbed my coat, and walked out of my office.

"Can you come over and help me?" Missouri asked, sounding desperate.

She didn't ask me to come over often, mostly because she didn't like me to see how messy her apartment always was. She didn't like to spend her time cleaning up because she preferred to spend her time doing things that were fun. I didn't mind a mess, but she was determined to keep that part of her chaotic personality private.

"I'll head there right now. Do you need me to stop at the store to get you anything?" I asked her as I reached the door.

"No, I already got way more than I need because I knew I'd ruin it all. I can't serve your mom bland or burnt cookies!" Her voice verged on a shriek, and I quickened my steps.

"Don't worry, I'll be there in a few minutes. Just... I don't know, take a break. You've been baking for days."

She'd been trying out every Christmas recipe she could find on Pin It that had the words *easy* and *simple* in the recipe listing.

"Okay, but hurry." She hung up without saying goodbye.

I was met with the scent of snow when I stepped out of the building. No flurries could be seen yet, but the weather was changing once again. A snowstorm was rolling in from the west, and the local news had announced it would be snowing heavily all weekend.

Missouri opened the door to her apartment ten minutes later with a look of absolute disgust on her face. "I hate cookies."

"Hi to you too." I patted the top of her head as I entered, and she closed the door behind me, leaning her back against it. Her apartment smelled like vanilla and pine, alluring to my senses, until I got a whiff of something that was possibly burning.

The heat of her apartment hit me right away, and I felt too warm in my coat. I shrugged it off and hung it on the back of the closet door, setting my shoes on the nearby mat.

"Remind me why you have to make Christmas cookies for my mom?" I asked, following her toward the kitchen.

"Because she makes all the food for us every year, and I want to be helpful," she said, turning to face me. "I'm turning twenty-four, and I'm still not able to contribute one meager morsel of a decent sugar cookie to the Christmas cause?" She threw her hands up, exasperated.

I rolled my eyes. She got a little dramatic when she became self-critical.

As I entered the kitchen, I stopped in my tracks, shocked to find what was waiting for us. Five messy cookie sheets were spread out over the small countertops. Flour and sugar spilled across every surface, including the floor. The sink overflowed with what looked like every bowl and mixing utensil my friend owned, and there were plates of sugar cookies beside the stove. Piping bags dripped blue and white frosting onto the counter, and an assortment of holiday-themed sprinkles blanketed the remaining counter space.

"What happened here?" I blinked at her, and she shrugged.

"I was baking." She pulled the sleeves of her maroon hoodie over her hands. "I guess I got carried away."

I arched a brow. "Just a little."

Avoiding the flour spill on the floor, I grabbed an angel-shaped cookie from a plate. The edges were a little browned, but I took a bite anyway.

Missouri watched closely as I chewed, and I could feel her willing the cookie to be good.

Once I swallowed, she asked, "Is it good?"

I winced, my throat feeling dry, but I swallowed again and said, "It's not bad."

She growled in frustration, making my lips pull up into a silent laugh.

"Okay, you need to take a break from the cookies," I said, placing the burnt cookie on the counter. With one hand placed against her back, I guided her out of the kitchen and away from the destruction that was strewn throughout the room.

When we reached the living room, which was a tiny space with one love seat, I saw multiple miniature Christmas trees and snow globes spaced out over the exposed wooden shelves to one side of the room. A small electric fireplace with an equally small mantel took up one wall, which Missouri had decorated with string lights and pine garland. A small tree stood in the wide entrance to the room—the only place it could fit—and we had to scoot around it to enter.

She plopped onto the middle of the beige loveseat, taking up the entire thing. Two red throw pillows bounced to the floor, and the last of the day's sunlight cast the room in a dim haze.

I watched as Missouri pouted, but I resolved to dig her out of the gloom. "We're getting out of here."

She looked up at me. "Why? It's almost dark out."

"Because you've been missing the kids at work, you're turning into a crazy baking lady, and you need some fresh air. We're going for a walk. Grab a jacket."

Her top lip curled up in a sneer, but she obliged, scooting around the Christmas tree and disappearing into her room. While I waited, I slid my finger across the books on the shelves, taking in the decorations that Missouri so perfectly set out for the holidays.

There were eleven snow globes in total lining one of the shelves, and each one had been a gift from me over the last eleven years. Inside every single one were two figures—a boy with tousled brown hair and a girl with long blonde waves. The globes varied in color and size, but the boy and girl inside them were always smiling together, no matter how snowy the scene was that they were set in.

I ran a hand through my hair and relaxed a little, the snow globes reminding me that we'd be alright no matter where we were. Even if Missouri went to NYU, I had faith that she'd always be my home.

"What're you doing?"

I spun around, startled. Missouri was standing beside the tree, her blue "outside" coat on, with a matching blue beanie. The pom-pom stuck up on top of her hat, and she slipped on her snow gloves.

"You scared me."

She shrugged her shoulders as she waited for an answer.

"I was looking at the snow globes. You're gonna like this year's," I said, unable to help the grin that appeared as I walked toward her.

"Whatever it looks like, I don't think it can top the one you got me last year." The sparkle in her eyes shifted in the light of the twinkling tree lights. "The little Purrseus? It's adorable. I have it by the couch."

I followed her finger as she pointed to the coffee table. Sure enough, the small snow globe was there. I turned it over, watching as the snow inside floated through the liquid, falling gently onto the cozy scene frozen in memory.

The scene inside was a rendition of my parents' living room, with the two of us seated on the couch, and Purrseus curled up in Missouri's arms. The figures were 3D printed, designed to look just like us. When I was seventeen, old enough to afford things without help from my parents, I started commissioning a snow-globe maker to create them.

I wanted the snow globes to be personalized, something that was just for me and her.

"I'm ready whenever you are." Missouri's voice entered my thoughts, and I followed her to the front door.

Once I had my coat and gloves on, we both slipped on our boots and headed outside.

Snowflakes were flurrying lazily from the sky, and the evening sun had already set, leaving us in darkness.

Missouri looked up and down the street. It was a cute little area of downtown, with small shops across the road and a children's park down the street.

"Come on," I said, wrapping my hand around hers.

She squeaked out a sound of joy as I tugged her along, both of us holding on tight to keep the other from slipping on the snowy sidewalk. I tried not to think too much about Missouri's hand in mine as we walked, but even through our thick gloves

I felt the heat of her—the way she affected me without intending to.

"Where are we going?" she whispered.

I leaned down, matched her quiet tone, and brought my lips close to her ear. "To the park."

I didn't miss the way she shivered or how her hand involuntarily tightened around mine.

"Is that where you're going to kill me?" she asked mockingly.

The corner of her lips pulled up.

"Nah," I said. "Too many variables. I wouldn't get away with it."

We continued whispering, as if the swirling snowflakes were listening to our evil plans.

"What are the variables?" she asked.

"The snow, for one." I looked back over our shoulders. "We're leaving footprints. That alone would give too much away."

"That's true," she added. "Where we came from, where you go after, your shoe size. You're right." She laughed. "You'd never get away with it."

I bumped her shoulder with mine. "Why are we whispering anyway?"

She looked around through the darkness. "It's just so... *still* out here. It feels too serene to mess it up by adding noise."

Although there were piles of snow all around us, the sidewalk was mostly clear. At least, it was until now. The falling snow had already created a thin layer of powder over the sidewalk.

At that moment, we arrived at the playground. The snow was much deeper here from previous snowfalls, but we trudged through it. Still holding Missouri's hand, I guided her to the swings, dusting the snow from two of them with my gloves.

When she sat, she released my hand. If we were dating, I wouldn't have had to let her go. It would have been normal to grab at her hand again, to have kept it in mine.

But we weren't dating, so I left the space between us empty.

Missouri rocked back and forth on the swing, and it creaked a little as the wet metal scraped against itself.

"I can't believe I only have a few weeks left here. What do you think you'll do when I'm gone?" Missouri asked, watching me closely.

I sat awkwardly on the small swing next to hers, rocking it slowly.

"I don't know," I answered honestly. "All my free time is spent with you. But I'm sure I'll figure it out. Maybe I'll join a gym or something like a normal guy." I gave her a wide smile to show her I was fine, but it didn't have the effect that I hoped.

She put her feet down, stopping her swinging motion. "If there was a good master's program here, you know I'd stay... or maybe I'll stay anyway." She shook her head. "I still haven't decided."

"Besides loving your job, what else could make you stay?" The question was out of my mouth before I could force it back down.

Her blue eyes stayed on mine. "I'm... not sure. Something special, I guess."

"Like, a guy?"

She giggled, averting her eyes. "Yeah, maybe a guy."

Was she talking about me? It's not like either of us hadn't dated before. She'd had boyfriends I'd liked and boyfriends I'd hated. I dated a girl once, but she wasn't Missouri. I didn't feel right about dating her, so I broke up with her.

I never told anyone the real reason why.

The thought of Missouri dating any more men that weren't me made my skin crawl and my stomach churn.

I cleared the lump from my throat. "Do you have someone in mind?" I asked.

We didn't talk about our relationships with each other, so I doubted she'd tell me if she had her eye on someone.

"Maybe I do." Her eyes filled with mischief, and she turned away from me, a smile playing at her lips.

"Who is it?" I couldn't help but ask, even though I didn't know if I wanted the real answer.

She kept her feet on the ground as she rocked the swing slowly back and forth. "I can't tell you."

My brows creased. "Why not? Do I know him?"

Please don't tell me it's someone I know.

"Yeah, you do actually."

I dropped my shoulders, then I realized I'd stopped swinging. So as not to let her see I was so deeply affected, I changed the subject.

"Are you cold? Ready to get back inside to work on those cookies again?"

Her brows scrunched, and she shook her head. "I think I have to give up on those."

"Why?" I'd never known Missouri to give up on a challenge when she had her mind set on it.

But she just shrugged, and bit her lower lip. I hated when she did that, so I kept my eyes on hers, fighting the urge to watch her mouth, wondering how soft her lips were.

"Because," she said, "I think I have to admit defeat this time. Cookies just aren't my thing. Maybe I can bring pancakes for Christmas breakfast?" Her smile shone bright in the dim light of a street lamp nearby.

"Yes, of course! I don't know why I hadn't thought of that before. You should make them the way you did last week. They were amazing," I said, and I watched as her smile grew at my reaction.

"You really think so?" she asked. "They're good enough to pair with your mom's cooking?"

"They're perfect," I said. "Everyone will love them, and they'll be so proud of you for stepping up in the culinary arts in your twenty-fourth year."

She laughed and rolled her eyes at me, giving me a playful shove that made my swing shake.

My mind drifted to last week when she spent the night at my house and how I woke up to her making pancakes in my kitchen and dancing in my clothes.

I still hadn't washed them. Sometimes I smelled the T-shirt, and then I wondered if I should feel weird about doing that. But I quickly pushed that idea away because I knew I'd continue doing it anyway.

I'd probably never wash it, so I could keep her scent close to me when she was no longer here.

Chapter Eight

Christmas was six days away, and I hadn't kissed Missouri yet. But every day that brought us closer to Christmas was a day that the energy in the air shifted, as if the weather itself knew something big was about to happen. It raised the hairs on my arms and made me acutely aware of everything around me.

If anyone was going to win Missouri's heart, it was me. Doubt tried to cloud my mind, cutting off the anticipation of a win, but I forced it away, banishing the dread that came with it.

I *would* win my best friend's heart. I had to. Otherwise, I'd be saying goodbye to her forever.

Missouri and I had history; our entire lives were twisted together at every angle.

A gut-wrenching thought followed me wherever I went. If she didn't want me after I confessed I loved her, then I'd have to walk away.

And that hurt more than anything.

I was starting to think I needed help on this one. I dialed my friend, Mark.

He answered on the first ring. "Hey, Jacob. What's goin' on?"

"Hey, man. I know we're all planning to get together tonight for Missouri's going away party, but do you think you could come over a little earlier? To talk?"

"Talk? Sure. Everything okay?" His baritone voice rang through the phone, and his question caused me to contemplate what I was about to ask.

I rubbed at the back of my neck. "Yeah, everything is fine. I just need a little advice."

Mark made a noncommittal noise. "I'm sure you're going to tell me later, but can I have a little heads up on what this advice pertains to? Do I get time to prepare?"

This made me laugh. "It's not a test, Mark. It's just a little something… about Missouri."

"Oh." He said this like he'd been waiting for it. Like he already knew what our conversation was going to be about.

I didn't question his remark. "Can you meet me at my place at six?"

"Sure. I'll be there. And I was going to text you about bringing something tonight. But since you called, is there some kind of food you want me to bring?"

I went through the list of attendees and what was already being brought. I shook my head.

"Nope, I think I got it all covered. Thanks, man."

"Of course, happy to help, bro. I'll see you tonight."

When he hung up, I looked at my phone. The time read one thirty-two in the afternoon. The day had gotten away from me quicker than I expected. I wanted my apartment to be spotless when I had it filled with our closest friends, so I spent the whole day cleaning.

I apparently lost track of time.

My first order of business was the party store. I'd decided

to make the party a mash-up of celebratory chaos. Christmas was around the corner, our birthday was always something to celebrate, and Missouri was going away, so she needed the excuse to see all our friends.

Chaos was Missouri's whole personality, in the best way. She'd love a chaotic party.

At the store, I purchased a large balloon bouquet in a mixture of colors ranging from red and green to sky blue and white. I also grabbed party plates that had a birthday cake printed on them and streamers that said *good luck*.

Next, I stopped at my parents' house.

I walked right in, not bothering to knock. My mom saw me right away, and a relieved smile spread over her face.

"There you are." She gave me a tight, motherly hug. "When I didn't hear from you all day, I thought maybe you forgot about the cake."

"How could I forget the cake?" I asked, giving her an incredulous look. "That's the best part. Sorry I didn't call. I've been running around town for the past hour, getting all the party supplies."

"What's up with your hair?" Mom asked, noticing the mess it had become from how I'd constantly run my hands through it.

"Nothing," I said, smoothing it down.

She grinned. "Just make sure you fix it up before the party tonight."

I grunted in response and headed to the kitchen. "So how did the cake turn out?" I asked her.

"Perfectly," she said, trailing after me.

We stopped in front of the counter, and Mom lifted the lid off a cake pan.

"It's vanilla on this side"—she pointed—"and chocolate on

this side. I know she likes both, so I didn't want her to be disappointed if it was just one."

I looked at the cake. Mom had written *Good luck at NYU* in red icing.

"Mom," I said, pausing before I continued. "What if she loves New York so much she doesn't come back?"

My mom's eyes searched mine, and after a moment, she finally spoke. "You love her, don't you?"

I nodded. "Yeah, of course I do. She's my best friend."

"No. I mean as *more*." Her voice was soothing, but it was asking the most basic question I hadn't answered out loud yet. "You've loved her for a long time, haven't you?"

I contemplated telling her no, that Missouri was just my friend. But I couldn't keep secrets from my mom. She could always tell if I was lying.

I nodded. "Yes, I do."

Mom's soft hand gently rested on my shoulder. "Jacob. Why didn't you ever tell me you had feelings for her?"

I shrugged. "I didn't tell anyone. I might love her, but… Mom, she might not feel the same way. She might reject me. So I thought the less people who knew my feelings, the better. I thought it would help ease the sting if everyone else didn't see it coming."

"Honey, you might have thought you were hiding it, but I've always known there was something more between you."

"But how?" I frowned, having thought I'd done a decent job of hiding my feelings for the past twelve years.

She looked to the ceiling and laughed quietly, more to herself than at me. "It's obvious you love her. Everyone knows."

My neck burned, and I knew my eyes were probably as wide as saucers. "Wha—who's everyone?"

"Me and your dad, Brad and Susan. Even some of your friends know."

My stomach plummeted. How would my friends know?

She must have seen my inner turmoil play across my face, because she turned and picked up the cake plate.

"Here," she said. "I don't want to keep you from getting ready for the party."

I was confused and worried about so many people knowing that I loved Missouri in case it all went downhill, but I took the plate from Mom. My mind was racing—foggy and overwhelmed at the idea of everybody watching me at the party tonight, knowing I was in love with my best friend this whole time.

Purrseus trotted into the kitchen with his fluffy gray tail swaying gracefully behind him. He rubbed his body against Mom's leg, and she bent down to scoop him into her arms. As she slid her hand down his back, the sound of his purring grew louder. It was surprisingly calming.

I reached out and rubbed under his chin. He closed his eyes and lifted his head, enjoying the attention.

We walked to the door, but before leaving, I turned back to my mom.

"How does everyone know I love Missouri?"

"It's written on your face, in your eyes. When you look at her, she's the star that you follow. You take care of her; you're her safe place where she can be herself. You've always been selfless, but when it comes to her, you're *more* than that." She placed a hand on my arm. "I'm proud of the man you are. You deserve someone as special as her."

At the sentiment, I became filled with renewed optimism. "Do you think she could love me back?"

Mom grew quiet for a moment as she thought. "I think you two are connected in a special way. You've known each other since the day you both were born." Her head tilted to the side as she continued. "You two are on one another's path for a reason. I don't believe lives intertwined like hers and yours can be easily separated."

I frowned, trying to understand what she was saying.

"Jacob," she said, "don't give up. No matter what, you're both going to make the right decisions. I trust that."

I smiled. "Thanks, Mom."

She kissed my cheek, and guided me out the door. I watched her as she stood on the porch, waving me away. The Christmas lights on the roof and porch blinked red and green, while the lights of the Christmas tree inside the window shined bright for passersby to enjoy.

I reversed out of the sloping driveway, the tires of my SUV crunching over a pile of ice. With my mind more stressed than ever, I drove back to my apartment to prepare.

At six, there was a knock on the door. I opened it, and Mark was standing in the cold, rubbing his bare hands together.

"Hey, man. Come on in," I said, waving him inside.

Mark walked in, his bulky six-foot-two-inch frame dwarfing me at my five foot eleven. As I closed the door, he looked around at the decorations visible in the living room. He removed his shoes without my asking him, which I appreciated.

He didn't waste a minute and got right to the point.

"So what did you need to talk about?" he asked, following me to the kitchen.

I shoved my hands in my jean pockets, feeling uncomfortable asking Mark for girl advice when the girl in question was Missouri.

"It's about Missouri." He nodded, and I forged ahead quickly. "I'm in love with her." My pulse raced at having finally said the words aloud to someone other than my mom. *That makes two people I've told in only one day.*

Mark blinked but didn't say anything. I took that as my cue to keep going.

"As you know, she's going away next month, and I need to tell her how I feel before she leaves. I've already been doing little things to show her how I feel, but I don't know what else to do."

He stood silent, but then his serious facade faded, replaced by a grin that spread across his whole face, forming tight lines by his light brown eyes. With one hand, he pumped a fist in the air.

"Finally!" he shouted, patting me on the back. It startled me, and I jumped, catching the gleam in his eye. "It's about time you did something about it."

"What does that mean?"

He laughed. "You've been hung up on Missouri forever. I was wondering when you'd decide to make a move."

"Make a—I'm not making a move," I stuttered. "That sounds so... brash."

"Whatever you want to call it, I'm glad it's finally happening."

"My mom was right," I muttered.

Mark lifted a brow. "What was that?"

"My mom. She said everyone already knew that I was in love with Missouri." I looked straight at him. "Is that true?"

"Well..." He shrugged his shoulders, like he didn't want to say one way or the other. But then he nodded, allowing me to have the truth. "We all knew. Eric, Claire, Jen. Even Elly and Samantha knew, and they're not the most attentive when it comes to gossip. Which is a good thing, because I know gossiping isn't right, but...Well, you get it."

I just watched as he rambled.

"We've all been rooting for you guys, hoping you both would see what you two have together."

An agreeable hum sounded in my throat, but I didn't feel as excited as he was about the situation. My nerves started to make their ugly appearance, and the tension in my shoulders was noticeable.

"Bro, what's wrong?" Mark clapped a large hand on my shoulder when he noticed my silence.

"I'm worried," I said.

"About what?"

"That she doesn't feel the same way." I looked up, and he leaned back against the kitchen counter, crossing his big arms in front of his chest. "I'm worried I've been coming on too strong. That I could be scaring her away. Or maybe... maybe she's never felt, and *will* never feel, more for me than just an innocent friendship. Bro, what if she just thinks of me like a brother?"

The thought hit me hard.

At one point in life, I did think of Missouri as my sister. We'd been together since we were children. She was a part of my life by default.

But then I turned twelve, and everything changed. The years came and went, and Missouri was still here. Still the same Missouri, only taller, funnier, prettier. We both grew up until my feelings were completely transformed. I no longer saw her as a sibling, but as the person I could spend the rest of my life with.

I could only hope that her feelings for me had evolved as well.

Having been so lost in my thoughts, I almost forgot Mark was standing there.

He shifted on his feet, then said, "You know what I think?"

I met his eyes, giving him permission to speak his mind.

"I think you're overthinking it."

A frown pulled at my eyebrows. "How so?"

"You're starting to freak yourself out, thinking about the worst-case scenario rather than the best case."

"Yeah," I said flatly. "Because the worst-case scenario is that I ruin everything by telling her my true feelings, and she never talks to me again. I could lose her over this."

"Or you could start something new and have forever with her." He uncrossed his arms. "It's just one of those risks you have to be willing to take. Ask yourself, *'is she worth the risk?'*"

"Yes," I said instantly. *She's worth everything.*

He tipped his head at me. "There's your answer."

"You're right," I said. "I was already going to tell her, but then I was having second thoughts."

"Don't have second thoughts."

I nodded. "I'm going to tell her."

I'd wanted to tell her for so long, but now the idea was solidified in my head. I had Mark to thank for it.

I decided I was going to tell her I love her on Christmas Day. No matter what happened leading up to it, whether she decided to keep her plans and go to NYU or not, I was telling her.

With Mark's words racing through my mind, I forgot about the time. Mark eyed the cake on the counter, then looked at the empty shopping bags and loose party streamers lying along the floor.

"Do you need some help with all this?" he asked encouragingly.

I checked the clock on the microwave—we had about forty minutes before everyone started showing up.

Mark helped me hang the rest of the streamers in the hallway, and he shook a bag of ice into a cooler to keep the cans of soda cold. I poured a few ingredients into a large bowl to make punch, and in a last-ditch effort to make my place extra cozy, I fluffed the decorative pillows on the couch. I'd never fluffed a pillow before, but the act of hitting them and tossing them down made me feel a little better.

At seven o'clock sharp, the doorbell rang, and when I opened the door, I lost my breath at the sight of Missouri.

Chapter Nine

Missouri was always beautiful. But tonight, she was drop-dead gorgeous, like she was a model who should have been on a runway somewhere.

Her blonde hair was in long loose curls that hung down the back of her white coat. She was wearing a dark green velvety dress underneath that rested above her knees and shimmered in the low light of the outdoor sconce. Black tights covered her legs, and she wore black boots that reached up her long calves.

"Hey." My voice came out almost like a whisper. My throat was dry, making it difficult to swallow.

Her smile was warm despite the cold outside.

"Hey," she said. Her lashes were long and black, and when she blinked at me, I could see the sparkle of her dark eyeshadow.

My mind shifted like a computer getting rebooted. There were so many tabs and apps shutting down and restarting that I couldn't seem to grab ahold of just one single thought. Nothing was loading properly, and I was grasping at information to keep myself afloat.

A loud, deep voice spoke from behind me, and Mark

pulled the door open wider. "Hey, Missouri! Come inside. It's cold out here," he said, like he was the one who lived here.

"Thanks." She smiled at him, and I moved aside, letting her in.

When I closed the door, I met Mark's gaze while Missouri wasn't looking. He frowned at me and pointed at her. From his slitted eyes, it was clear he was wondering why I froze in the doorway and didn't welcome her inside.

I frowned back, shrugging my shoulders. While Missouri was unzipping her tall boots, Mark pointed at her again, gesturing for me to take her coat.

"Hey, Missouri, let me take your coat," I said, trying but failing to sound normal.

Just be normal, Jacob. She's going to see that you're acting totally weird.

"Thanks," she said.

When she shrugged out of her white jacket, the back of her velvet dress revealed itself, which in turn revealed a lot of her back. My stomach somersaulted at the sight, even though the only skin showing was her narrow, toned back. Long sleeves hugged the length of her arms.

My brain skipped like a scratchy record. Mark cleared his throat, and I shook myself out of my stupor. Thankfully, Missouri didn't notice as she looked around at the decorations.

"I'll just take this to my room." I grabbed Missouri's coat from her, and she smiled her thanks.

When I reached the end of the hall, I heard footsteps following, then Mark entered my room behind me.

"Bro, what is going on with you?" he asked. "You're acting so weird."

I ran a hand through my hair. "Did you see how she looks tonight? I can't focus."

He frowned. "Yeah, she's beautiful. But you already knew

that. You're her best friend; you see her all the time. How is tonight any different?"

"I don't know. Maybe it's because today, for the first time ever, I admitted to loving my best friend to not one, but to *two* people. And I found out that everyone I know, including all the people who will be here tonight, already knows it! That's a lot of pressure on me."

I stuck my head out the door to make sure no one was in the hall where they could hear me. I couldn't see Missouri, but voices drifting from the kitchen told me others had arrived.

"Okay," said Mark. "I can see how that would be a lot of pressure. But no one is going to say anything to you about it. They don't know that you know that they know." He frowned, thinking through the logic of what he just said. Satisfied, he nodded. "So just act normal. If it makes you feel better, I'll stay away from you guys tonight. You know, since I know that you know I know…"

I narrowed my eyes at him, trying to make sense of his words. I sighed. "You're right. Everything is the same. Nothing's changed. I'm the only one freaking out and being weird."

"You'll be fine. Let's just get back out there." He nodded his head toward the door, and when I told him I'd follow in a minute, he left the room to join the rest of the guests.

I was still clutching Missouri's coat. Bringing it up to my nose, the scent of her coconut shampoo clung to the fabric, calming my racing mind. My pulse slowed. The way my body responded to her was evidence that everything was okay.

Missouri was still here for now, and everything was going to be fine.

❄

Half-empty paper cups lined the kitchen counter. The cake, which was served only ten minutes ago, was almost gone. I was pretty sure Eric ate three pieces, and I knew for a fact that Missouri had two—one chocolate and one vanilla.

We'd all gathered around my living room to play Charades. The air was warm from body heat, and my chest filled contentedly at having all our closest friends gathered together so close to Christmas. From the corner of the room, the lights on the tree shone brightly. More than one person had commented on the orange-and-popcorn garland, and I was proud to brag on Missouri and her wonderful decorating ideas.

Her elbow gently brushed against my side as we sat on my couch. Claire and Samantha were on Missouri's other side, while I sat as close to the arm rest as I could get to make room. Jen stood in front of the small unlit fireplace, miming something the rest of her team was supposed to guess. The teams were split into boys versus girls; however, since there were five girls and only three boys, Missouri volunteered to be on the boys' team.

Jen mimed something shooting up from the ground, spreading her hands in the air.

Mark shouted, "*Rocket*," and everyone squawked at him that he was helping the wrong team.

"Fireworks!" Elly said, raising her voice over the clamor of the others.

"Yes!" Jen pointed at her with a wide smile on her face, then sat on the floor near the doorway, moving her legs so Mark could act out his word next.

He grabbed a slip of paper out of the basket on the coffee table, opened it, and looked at it for several seconds without blinking.

"Ready?" I asked.

He nodded at me, and I started the three-minute timer on my phone.

Mark's hand pulled an invisible item out of his pocket, and then he pretended to riffle through whatever he was holding.

Eric shouted, *"Wallet,"* and I offered a guess, asking if it was *money*.

Mark ignored us, pretending next to pull something out of the invisible item in his hand, tapping it in the air.

"You're paying for something!" I shouted, moving to the edge of my seat.

"Bro, you're good at this," Mark said, giving me a fist bump. He moved back to his spot in the doorway, this time sitting on the floor beside Jen.

Missouri's cheeks were rosy from the excitement. "Nice job, Mark," she said. "And you too, Jacob." She turned to me, and I noticed how close our faces were. I could have easily kissed her.

I smiled. "Thanks. I think it's your turn next."

I patted her on the knee, and her eyes locked onto mine. For a second I could imagine that we were alone—that it was just the two of us sharing the same tiny corner of my couch in a world full of billions of square feet of space.

But I remembered quickly that we weren't alone, and I dropped my hand from her leg, a blush creeping along the back of my neck.

She stood and moved to the front of the room. For an instant, her eyes met mine again, but then she grabbed a slip of paper from the basket, and I started the timer.

Right away, Missouri went through the motions of pulling something over her head and onto her face.

Someone guessed that her word was *mask*, but she shook her head.

"Goggles!" I yelled confidently.

"Yeah," she said, beaming. "That's the winning point, right?"

"No fair," said Samantha. "You two are always winning."

I looked at Samantha with a playful grin, putting my hands out placatingly. "Sorry, Samantha. It's not our fault we're so in sync."

"You can say that again," said Eric from where he was leaning against the wall, his lips pulled up in amusement. "You two have been like this since before any of us even met you. You're, like, the exact same person."

I looked at Missouri to catch her reaction. She watched everyone from under her eyelashes like she was embarrassed of the attention.

"Oh, guys," she said playfully, "don't be jealous. It's not our fault that we can read each other's minds. It's just the Christmas gift that keeps on giving."

"Right, because you were both born on Christmas." Samantha's eyes brightened when she looked between the two of us. "What are you going to do when Missouri goes to New York, Jacob?"

My pulse quickened. "I—"

"We're not really thinking about it yet," Missouri interrupted. Her blue eyes met mine, reassuring me. "We're enjoying the time we have together right now, looking forward to the holiday this week, and turning twenty-four together."

When I looked at the group of friends in my living room, I saw a mix of feelings on each face. Jen and Claire looked like they didn't believe a word she said. Mark and Eric were looking at each other, like they knew more than they were letting on. And Elly and Samantha had hearts in their eyes as if they knew my secret.

With my heart in my throat, I tried willing this conversation away, no longer feeling comfortable now that Missouri's impending departure was the topic of conversation.

"I'm going to get another drink. Anyone want one?" I stood from the couch, and Mark and Eric accompanied me into the kitchen. The sound of the girls giggling followed on our heels.

"So," said Eric, "what are you going to do about that?" He pointed his thumb over his shoulder toward the living room, his caramel-colored skin popping brightly against his yellow knit sweater.

I scooped my finger against the leftover icing on the cake plate, then licked my finger. Mom's homemade cream-cheese icing was the best I'd ever tasted.

"Do about what?" I asked, pretending I didn't know what he was referring to.

"Come on, Jacob," said Mark, stepping closer. "He knows too."

I rolled my eyes. "Of course he does."

Eric watched our interaction. "Have you guys talked about this?" he asked, motioning between us.

Mark crossed his arms, his black T-shirt stretching over his biceps. The guy spent most of his life in the gym, and it showed. Thankfully, he kept his voice low. "Jacob asked for a little advice on his next steps."

If anyone else were hearing this conversation from the outside, they'd probably think I was joining an AA meeting or something.

Eric took a swig from a random cup on the counter. I wasn't totally convinced that it belonged to him.

"So you, what? Told him how to win the girl? Dude, you already have her. She's so goo-goo-eyed over you."

At that, my mood lightened. "You think so?"

"One hundred percent. She's never looked at another guy the way she looks at you. Not even the guys she's dated."

I rolled my eyes at the mention of her exes. "Don't even bring those guys up. None of them deserved her."

"Whoa, watch out for Jacob," Mark said teasingly. His rumbling laughter caused his muscular arms to shake. "Are you jealous?"

"No," I scoffed. "None of them had what she and I have. There was never any competition."

"Right. But *you* never dated her." Eric's words weren't mean—they were just the truth.

Silence followed, and I released a heavy breath.

"Yeah," I said. "You're right. But I'm doing my best to change that."

Chapter Ten

After the party, Missouri insisted on staying to help clean up. Samantha and Elly shed a few tears as she walked them to the door, and Mark gave her a bear hug, almost lifting her off the floor. She giggled and smiled, thanking them all for coming and promising to send them all a text when she settled at NYU.

There wasn't much to do around the apartment, but Missouri busied herself anyway by wiping the countertops and taking down the decorations while I collected the trash. Her Christmas playlist played through my Bluetooth speaker while we worked, and she bobbed her head and moved her shoulders to the beat of *Santa Claus Is Coming to Town*.

It was getting late, but with her here, I wasn't ready to end the night.

As she covered the remainder of the cake, I sat on a stool at the kitchen counter.

"Thanks for putting this together," she said cheerfully. "The party was a lot of fun."

The joyful memory of her earlier laughter played in my ears, the soundtrack to a perfect day.

"Of course. I'm glad you were able to spend some time with the girls before you leave. I heard a lot of laughing. What did the girls talk about when the guys weren't around?"

She turned to me, putting her hip against the edge of the counter. "Just girl stuff."

"Just girl stuff?" I repeated, raising a playful brow at her. "You're not going to tell me?"

"Are you a girl?"

"Obviously not."

"Then I can't tell you."

My eyes roamed down her body, caught on the shimmer of her green dress. I averted my gaze, focusing on a pile of unused paper plates and willing my focus to stay there.

I'd seen her dressed up before, but she'd never stood in *my* kitchen looking as good as *this*. She was so beautiful, it physically hurt to keep my hands off her.

And how I wanted to put my hands all over her, through her hair, and down the soft sleeves of her dress.

Missouri lifted a glass of water to her lips, then sat on the stool next to me. "You might have heard the girls, but I didn't hear the guys at all. What were you all whispering about?"

"We weren't whispering."

She gave me a straight face. "Mark is usually the loudest of the group, and I hardly heard him at all for a good twenty minutes. You were definitely whispering about something." Her eyes widened, and she leaned forward to give me her best puppy-dog face. "Tell meee."

With a playful shove, I rested my palm on her forehead and pushed her away. "Get out of here," I laughed.

"I know you want to tell me," she said, pinching my side and giggling.

"Hey!" I captured her hand in mine, and the contact felt too good.

Sparks flew instantly. She laughed lightly, but her playful countenance faded as her eyes looked down at our joined hands.

I couldn't stop myself, and I gave in to the desire I'd had all night, slowly brushing my other hand up the soft sleeve of her dress. The lines in her face softened as I watched for signs of disapproval, but I found none. She shuddered with pleasure, and her eyes followed every movement of my hand as it trailed higher up her arm. My fingertips traveled past her forearm, up to her shoulder.

The music on the wireless speaker changed to *All I Want for Christmas Is You*, wrapping around us and pulling us closer.

When my fingers trailed over the smooth exposed skin on her shoulder, she tilted her head, revealing more of her delicate neck. With a light touch, I brought my fingertips to her chin, and her eyes closed.

I brought my face close to her ear, until we were just inches apart.

"Missouri." My voice was no more than a whisper.

She leaned her body closer to mine. "Mm-hmm…" she hummed. Her eyes remained closed, and her brows raised in question.

"I really want to kiss you," I admitted, tilting her chin toward me ever so gently while moving my lips from her ear to brush lightly over her jaw.

She raised her mouth toward mine, leaning closer as if she were inviting me to do exactly what I wanted.

I edged forward on the stool, drawing my body closer to hers and framing her legs between mine.

I pressed a kiss to her jaw, and she breathed in deeply. Then I pressed another closer to her mouth, but not quite on her lips. She didn't move away when the corners of our lips brushed.

Without a dismissal, my resolve to kiss her was bolstered. I laid my lips on hers, and she sighed through her nose, relaxing into me like she'd been waiting for this.

Missouri's lips pressed back against mine, gentle and hesitant. I couldn't believe I was finally kissing Missouri Bellview.

I didn't expect to show her my true feelings today, but my Christmas timeline was dwindling. I was taking every chance I had, using it to show her I loved her.

Her mouth parted slightly, and I kissed her bottom lip. It was full and soft, just like I imagined it would feel. As I savored the taste of her peppermint Chapstick, her hand held mine tighter while her other hand slid around the back of my neck. Goosebumps formed on my arms from her touch, and I pressed my mouth more firmly against hers as our kiss deepened.

There was no way I could ever go back to the life I knew before this kiss. It undid me, and I was determined to make it happen again. And again. And again.

Seconds passed that felt like minutes, and yet when the kiss ended, it still felt far too soon. Missouri leaned away first, removing her hand from my neck and putting a few inches of space between us. One of my hands still held onto hers, and her chin rested against the other.

I lowered my hand from her face to rest it on my thigh, and Missouri's blue eyes scanned mine. Her chest rose and fell in quick succession, her lungs working to replace the breath that I stole.

"That was... something," she said, a smile tugging at her lips.

Oh, how I wanted to put my lips back on that smile.

"Was it okay?" I asked. I realized I sounded like a teenager who'd just had their first kiss. But with Missouri, I wanted it to be perfect.

She squeezed my hand, and I squeezed back three times.

"It was… unexpected," she said quietly.

I pulled back. "I'm sorry. I know I didn't—"

"Unexpected, but not unwelcome." Her eyes sparkled as she watched for my reaction, something playful hanging around her lips.

I couldn't help but smile. "Missouri, I like you. A *lot*," I breathed.

Her brows creased. "I like you too, Jacob, but I'm going to New York. Trying something like this between us… it might have to wait."

My heart plummeted from the mountaintop it had just climbed. "I know the timing isn't great, but I was thinking… What if I go with you to New York?"

"You already are. To drop me off."

"No, I mean to live there while you're taking your classes."

Her eyes widened in shock, and she pulled her hand back from mine. "Jacob, I can't ask you to do that. You have a life here." She stood from the stool and walked around the kitchen island to stand on the opposite side.

I stood too, hands flat on the countertop. "My life is you, Missouri. It doesn't matter where you are. If I'm with you, then I'm living. Staying here without you… It wouldn't be a life anymore."

"I don't know." She rubbed at her forehead.

"I can get a job as an accountant anywhere," I said, trying to sway her, to help her see how serious I was about trying. "I can go with you. I can get a job, an apartment of my own. We can see each other all the time."

"It feels too fast." Her eyes shifted, like they were asking me for answers to questions she didn't know how to ask.

"We've spent our whole lives together already. You're my best friend, my person. You *know* me." I scanned her eyes, hoping I could convince her that this was right.

On the other side of the counter, she ran her hands through the length of her hair, shaking her head. "I don't know," she repeated. "It's all too overwhelming right now. A new city, a new school, starting college again. I can't do all that with a new boyfriend too. We need to take this slow."

For me, the past twelve years had been excruciatingly slow. But I didn't say that.

Instead, I said, "We can go as slow as you need to. I just know that we're going to make it work."

Her smile was tentative, but I could see that she wanted to believe me.

"Just to be clear, I'll do anything to make us work," I reiterated. "Just try and see where this goes. Me and you."

She chewed on her bottom lip, and I smiled, finally knowing what it felt like to have it against my own lips.

"I need time to think about it. It's just a lot to take in, and a lot of big changes are happening right now," she finally said.

I walked around the counter to join her and took her hands in mine.

Smiling down at her as she looked up at me, I said, "I was going to wait until Christmas Day to make my move, but..." I smirked. "You look so breathtakingly beautiful in that dress, I've been wanting to kiss you all night. The moment finally got the better of me."

"Oh, this old thing?" She blushed slightly as she smoothed her hand down her dress. "Thank you. But, why wait until Christmas Day?" she asked, a smile growing on her lips.

I shrugged. "Besides the obvious—Christmas and our joint birthday—I think there's something special about that day. Something magical."

Her expression softened, and she wrapped her arms around my middle, resting her cheek against my chest. I held her close, enjoying the warmth of her body against mine.

"You're okay with me taking time to think about all this?" she asked into my chest.

"Take all the time you need. I'll always be right here."

Our kiss played over and over in my mind on repeat. I kissed Missouri Bellview, and it was everything I ever imagined and hoped it would be.

And she kissed me back. I knew there were fears and stressors floating around in her head, but she didn't pull away. She didn't run.

Chapter Eleven

"Are we still on for Christmas Eve movie night?" Missouri asked, her sleepy voice sounding through my car speakers.

I was on my way to work, and I was shocked to see her calling this early when she had nowhere to be. If I were her, I would have been sleeping in, but I was happy to start my day talking to her.

"Of course," I replied. "Why wouldn't we do movie night?"

"No reason. Just making sure."

I was relieved that she wanted to do the same things we always did, keeping in tune with our traditions. We went to my parents' house yesterday to see Purrseus, and we had dinner with Mom and Dad. She hadn't acted strange or different since our kiss, but she also hadn't kissed me again either, and we hadn't talked about it.

The whole world continued to spin on its axis, life going on as normal, while I was falling over, losing my balance. To me, everything had already changed.

But when it came to Missouri, she was acting like nothing

was different. And I couldn't seem to grasp what that meant for us.

"Dinner's at six with our parents, and then they're going to the movies to see that new Christmas comedy that just came out," I said. Frost still covered part of my window, and I adjusted the vents to clear it away.

"Christmas All the Way?" Her excited voice carried through the car, warming me more than the heat blowing through the vents. "I wanted to see that. I'm surprised our dads are interested in it at all—it doesn't seem like their kind of movie."

Every year on Christmas Eve, both our families had dinner at my mom and dad's house, followed by a movie night. Mom and Dad went out with Brad and Susan to see something in the theater, while Missouri and I stayed back to watch something at the house. When we were kids, we would go with them, but the movie always had to be family friendly, so it was more for us than for them.

But when we got old enough to stay home alone, we offered for our parents to use that night as a double date night. They invite us to come along every year, but we agreed years ago that we felt like the third wheel. So, in keeping the Christmas Eve movie night tradition going, Missouri and I continued to watch something together at my parents' house.

"Do you want to go with them?" I asked. "I don't mind. We can change up our plans this year." I'd honestly hate to give up our movie night together, but I was willing to do whatever made her happy.

"No," she said right away. "We don't have to do that. I'll see it another time or wait until it streams on TV. Have you decided what we're watching at the house?"

I was glad she didn't want to go with the parents. I sifted through movie ideas I had in mind. "There's *The Grinch*, which is always a classic."

"Purrseus doesn't like that one."

"Right, *Purrseus* doesn't like it." I rolled my eyes, although she couldn't see me, and smiled.

"He doesn't. It has a dog."

Her voice came through the speakers so matter-of-factly that I chuckled.

"Okay, Misery. Whatever you say."

She groaned.

"Next up on the list is *Home Alone*."

"Nooo," she practically whined.

"What's wrong with *Home Alone*?"

"Besides the fact that a child is alone in the city being chased by two adult men? Nothing. Absolutely nothing is wrong with that movie."

Something like a snort came out of my nose.

Missouri sputtered. "Did you just snort?" She laughed at me, and the sound was so melodic, I didn't mind that I was the subject of her laughter.

If I had a nickel for every time her laugh turned my stomach upside down, I'd be extremely rich. I'd buy a mansion and give it right back to her. I would tell her I bought her a home paid for with the sound of her own beautiful laughter.

When she finally stopped laughing, I said, "You're right. That's a terrible movie."

"Thank you for saying I'm right," she said cheerfully. Dishes clinked in the background.

"Don't get a big head," I said in a flat tone, even though I was smiling. "Moving on, we have *The Santa Clause*."

"Yes."

"So quick to agree to that one?" I asked.

"There's absolutely nothing wrong with that movie," she quipped. I heard water running and assumed she was probably washing dishes.

I hummed thoughtfully. "Okay, you're right. Again."

"Yes! I love when I'm right." Her smile was practically palpable through the phone. "*And* I love that movie. Wait, is there a dog in that one?"

"Actually, I don't remember."

"Oh, well," she said. "We'll cover Purrseus's eyes if there is. By the way, are you almost at work yet?"

"I'm just pulling in." I parked outside my office building, hating that I had to say goodbye to her. "Want to hang out later?"

"What did you have in mind?" A sputtering sound could be heard in the background, and I knew her coffee maker was brewing her morning roast.

"We haven't driven around to see the Christmas lights yet, so I was thinking we could go right after work?"

"That sounds fun. What about dinner?" Missouri's voice transferred from the car speakers to my phone, and I held it to my ear.

"Don't worry about that," I replied, already having something in mind. "I'll pick up something." I grabbed my backpack that held my laptop and swung it over my opposite shoulder. "I'll run home to grab a few things, then meet you at your apartment?"

"That's perfect. Can't wait."

"Great. Be prepared to have fun."

I logged out of my work computer and rushed through the hall to get home. When I arrived, I ran around grabbing things from the kitchen, changed into comfortable sweats, found a festive winter hat, and headed back out.

Missouri stepped out the door right when I pulled into the

lot of her apartment complex.

With a scarf bundled around her neck and wearing a bright red beanie that matched her mittens, she walked down the front walkway toward me. Two blonde braids hung over her shoulders, and she wore dark green sweatpants tucked into tan UGG boots.

I rolled down the window and leaned over the console to shout in an annoyingly loud voice, "Uber for Misery Bellview?"

An older man walking his dog nearby stared at us as he passed.

Missouri rolled her eyes, opening the passenger door. "You're so embarrassing," she said in way of greeting.

I sat back in my seat with a grin, and she slid in.

"But you love it," I said. "What would you do without me?"

"I'd probably be less self-conscious because you wouldn't hang around embarrassing me." Her lips tugged into a smirk as she narrowed her eyes at me.

I leaned closer. "In other words, your life would be boring."

She laughed, pushing me away. "Sure, we'll go with that."

Missouri connected her phone to the car and acted as DJ as we drove. All our favorite Christmas songs played, and we danced around, heads bopping to the music. It hadn't snowed in a few days, but the cold outside kept the snowdrifts piled high near the edges of the road.

After a few minutes, we pulled into a neighborhood known for their extravagant light display. Each house on the street participated in the free drive-through event, and every night from Thanksgiving to New Years, the street was lined with family-filled cars who came to enjoy the show.

Six years ago, the street was officially renamed North Pole Avenue.

A sign near the entrance to the street listed a radio channel, and I tuned the radio so we could hear the music that played in sync with the light show.

Every house was covered in lights. Large inflatable figures —snowmen, The Grinch, and even a few Santa Clauses— graced most of the yards. There were blinking lights wrapped around trees and lining sidewalks. Large candy canes stuck out of the snow, and life-sized gingerbread men stood at attention on one side of the road, their mouths lit up and synced to the music. They looked like they were singing along with the other singing figures.

"You know," said Missouri, resting her feet on the dash, "I heard that if someone on this street sells their house, the next person to move in has to sign an agreement saying they'll contribute to the light show every year."

"Really?" I looked over at her. "That's crazy."

"Yeah," she chuckled. "I imagine it would be a lot of responsibility as a homeowner here. This light show is no joke."

"Not to mention the electricity bills at the end of the season."

Her eyes grew wide. "You're right. I hadn't even thought of that part." She turned back to watch the lights as we passed, singing joyfully along to the music.

I drove us slowly down the street so we could take it all in.

"Oh, check behind your seat," I said, remembering what I brought.

Missouri pulled a black cooler bag onto her lap. "What is it?"

"Open it."

She pulled her feet back to sit with her legs crossed under her and unzipped the bag, pulling out two thermoses.

Holding one in each hand, she looked at me. "What's inside?"

"Just open them and find out," I said, chuckling lightly at her inquisitive nature.

She unscrewed the lid on the first thermos, and her eyes went dreamy the moment the scent hit.

"You brought hot cocoa?" Her smile warmed my insides more than any hot cocoa could.

"I did. Just for you." I nodded toward the other thermos. "Open that one."

I brought the car to a halt, waiting for the line of vehicles ahead of me to begin moving again. I didn't mind the traffic through the street—it gave me a chance to look at Missouri.

She opened the second thermos. When she saw and smelled what was inside, her eyes flashed to mine. "You didn't," she said, her face awestruck.

"I did," I said, my smile stretching. "Again, just for you."

Inside the thermos was her favorite cheddar-and-broccoli soup. It wasn't the most romantic gesture or the most lavish meal, but I knew it would make her feel special.

"Jacob, why are you so perfect?" She leaned her head back and looked at me.

I nodded. "You're welcome."

Missouri reached out to hug me, but the spacing in the car was awkward and the console dug into my ribs as I leaned toward her. I caught a whiff of her coconut shampoo when she wrapped her arm around my neck, and my hand moved around her back.

While someone might have given a friend a hug and quickly broken away, this hug lingered. Missouri didn't let go, and I wasn't willing to be the first one to make this moment end. It was too good, too perfect, the way her chin rested on my shoulder, the feel of her breath on the back of my neck.

Through the front window, red brake lights disappeared, but I hardly noticed. My best friend turned her face slightly toward mine, moving so slowly it was killing me inside. I thought she might kiss me.

A horn honked behind us, making us jump. Missouri pulled back from me, and I rested my hands on the steering wheel, noticing for the first time that the line of cars had moved on ahead of us.

I raised my hand in an apologetic wave to the driver behind me.

"Sorry," I said, although there was no way they could hear me. Missouri cackled, and I smiled as I drove forward.

After a moment, I glanced over at Missouri. She sifted through the remaining contents of the cooler bag, fishing out a spoon for the soup.

And because I knew all of Missouri's facial expressions, it was obvious to me she was fighting a smile.

A big one.

Chapter Twelve

On Tuesday night, I found myself wishing I had stayed home from this particular family event.

It wasn't a long-standing tradition, per se, but Missouri attempted to get me on the ice at least once a year. So here I was at the ice rink.

Which I hated.

And she knew it.

"Alright, let's do this." Missouri finished tying her skate and stood, as effortless as ever. She eyed me with an upturned brow. "Do you need help?"

I stepped toward her, fumbling slightly. "No, I'm good." I frowned, already knowing I wouldn't enjoy a single part of this activity.

"Come on, I'll help you." She walked to me without a problem, the blades of her skates hardly making any sound against the ground.

She might as well have been floating—her movements were as graceful as an angel's.

"Just put your arm over me, and I'll hold you here," she

said, sliding her hand around my back to grip the side of my coat.

I did as she suggested, resting my arm over her shoulder.

She helped me walk the few feet to the edge of the rink while I tried to ignore the stares of other skaters around us. I wobbled like a newborn giraffe, which was not something I was proud of.

When we reached the ice, she stepped on first, and I was forced to follow. My skates slid out awkwardly as soon as my weight shifted to the ice. Missouri didn't let go of me, and I kept my arm draped over her shoulders. A wave of embarrassment washed over me, but I was grateful for the assistance.

"Now the fun part," I mumbled, taking another step on the ice. My body involuntarily stiffened as I unsteadily inched myself along.

"It will be fun," she said back. "I promise."

I harrumphed. "You say that every year."

She stared up at me, her eyes shining under the lights of the rink. "And every year, you have fun."

I turned my face away, fighting the urge to lean down and kiss her perfect lips.

We were outside in the freezing cold, there were three days until Christmas, and I could think of ten other things I'd rather be doing right now.

My foot slipped to the side, but Missouri held me upright, her grip around me tightening.

We did a lap around the rink, doing our best to avoid the children who sped past.

"Insufferable," I growled, nearly losing my footing.

Her lips formed a wide smile, and her eyes got a faraway look. "Can you imagine doing this at Rockefeller Center?"

I winced. "No, I can't imagine," I said through my teeth.

Her hand wrapped around my waist tickled my side, and I lurched. "Hey, don't do that! You'll make me fall."

"Then don't be so serious," she said with a chuckle.

"You know I hate skating." I looked down at her. "I don't have good balance."

"I know. You're always falling, even *off* the ice."

"No, I'm not." I frowned, but my heart skipped as I played into our little game.

"Yes, you are, Jacob." She looked up at me, and my smile gave me away. Her knowing eyes got unbelievably wide. "Stop. You're always teasing me!" A playful tone rang through her words. "I'm about to drop you right here."

She started to pull away from me, but I grabbed her hand in mine, holding it tightly against my side so her arm stayed around me.

"Don't leave me."

Her smile faded as she searched my eyes. The air shifted, but I couldn't put my finger on what had happened.

"Okay," she said. "I won't."

We skated around the rink three more times before I was begging her to let me get off the ice.

"Fine," she said. "I guess you did enough laps for your yearly penance." She laughed at her own joke. I raised a brow at her, but she ignored me.

When we got to the side of the rink, I grabbed onto the wall for dear life. I couldn't wait to step off the ice where I could finally get these deadly shoes off me.

"Why do you enjoy this, anyway?" I asked her. I was slightly out of breath, from both risking my life out there and from being close to Missouri the whole time.

"Because you're so good at everything, except this. It's nice to see you're not really Superman. That you have a kryptonite." She leaned in, like she was sharing a secret. "And maybe because when we go ice skating, I like getting to hold onto you."

Before I realized what was happening, she reached up and pressed a featherlight kiss to my cheek, one that spread heat through my body. She backed away, dropping her arm from around my waist. I gripped the half wall for support as she glided off with an ease I could only envy.

My pulse raced from her admission, and I stood stunned, frozen against the wall.

I turned so many thoughts over in my head, but only one thought took precedence, shining brightly in big green letters that blinked and flashed like the lights strung over the rink.

She *liked* me.

It sounded so juvenile, but it was everything. Twelve-year-old me would have been fist-pumping the air at that realization.

It was the turning point between just friends and something more. Our kiss meant something to her. And apparently, holding me while we skated meant something to her too.

I watched from my perch at the wall as Missouri reached the opposite side of the rink. She spun her body until she was moving backward, swaying her hips to move her skates along the ice. Her movements were light and elegant, yet she looked strong and powerful.

Her eyes met mine across the distance, and she smiled. It was a playful, teasing smile that I loved. The one that told me we had a secret between us that only we knew.

I smiled back.

When Missouri's parents found us an hour later, we were sitting at an outdoor picnic table near the concession stand.

Missouri was nursing a cup of hot cocoa, and I picked at a soft cinnamon-sugar pretzel that we shared between us.

Mrs. Bellview leaned down to kiss her daughter on the cheek, then ruffled my hair, like she did when I was ten. "Hey, guys, are you having fun?" she asked.

"Hey, Mrs. Bellview," I said. "Missouri is having a ton of fun."

"Oh?" Her eyebrows raised in question. "Are you not having fun, Jacob?"

Missouri bumped my shoulder with hers. "Jacob doesn't like ice skating."

Her mom frowned. "I'm sorry to hear that. If you don't like it, why do you come with us every year? We'd understand if you chose not to come."

My shoulders rose. "Because Missouri likes it."

I looked at her, and she blushed, covering it by sipping her hot cocoa.

"Well, that's very kind of you," Mrs. Bellview said, looking between the two of us.

Mr. Bellview walked up and took a seat next to Missouri while her mom stepped away to stand in line at the concession stand.

"So, who's up for a little race?" asked Missouri's dad. He leaned his arms on the table, looking expectantly at both of us.

Missouri shook her head. "No thanks, Dad."

"Missy, come on. Me and you." Mr. Bellview nudged her playfully with his elbow. "They're about to start the adult races."

Every year, when the town put the ice rink together in the downtown plaza, they incorporated fun activities into the rink schedule. Those usually included a kids' dance party with Santa on the ice, a reindeer petting zoo just outside the rink, and races for all ages to participate. Tonight, they were hosting the adult race.

The first person to skate from one side of the rink to the other was declared the winner. They received a cheap trophy as well as bragging rights until the next year.

"Not this time. You should do it alone." Missouri's voice was kind, but I could see from the crease in her brow that she was expecting him to keep bugging her about it.

He frowned. "Why not? What's wrong?"

"I just..." she started, looking increasingly uncomfortable. "I'm not very competitive."

"I know that, and we don't have to win."

I watched quietly.

Missouri looked at her dad, her features softening. "We don't?"

He rested his hands on the table in front of him, palms open. "I mean, sure, it would be nice to win. But it's not everything."

"That's not what you usually say." Missouri's voice was quiet, like she was afraid to speak her mind. "I don't like to do competitions with you because you treat me like one of your football players when you're under pressure. You just get loud and expect me to follow your lead."

I turned my attention away from them, giving them some semblance of privacy. The thought occurred to me that maybe I should have left them alone, but I knew Missouri—she hated conflict. I thought she would want me to stay nearby.

Mr. Bellview's voice lowered into something gentle. "I know I can get a little carried away when it comes to competing," he said. "And I know I've been a little hard on you because of it."

"A little?" Missouri commented.

"A lot," he corrected himself. "But I've never meant to take the fun out of competing. Games, competition—it should be fun. And I guess I've made my profession around an intense game that made me forget that."

From the corner of my eye, I saw him slip his hand over Missouri's.

"I'm sorry for treating you like a football player," he continued. "But I'm even more sorry for treating you as anything less than the most special daughter a man could ask for."

"Thank you." Missouri hugged him, and he wrapped his large arms around her. He kissed the top of her head, and I took that moment—now that I knew she was okay—to look for my own parents.

I peered through the crowd of skaters on the ice, grateful to not have those awful skates on anymore. I spotted my parents, hand in hand and smiling as they glided somewhat clumsily on the ice. My mom's skating looked more controlled than my dad's—who was half walking, half skating—and I realized where I got my clumsiness from.

Mom spotted me, waved, and guided Dad to the half wall where I stood.

"Jacob, are you done skating?" Mom asked when they reached me.

I made an exaggerated sigh. "Yes, thanks to everything that is good in this world. If I'm lucky, I won't have to endure that again for another year."

Dad let out a hearty laugh. "I know what you mean. If it weren't for your mom, I'd be out of here."

I smirked, and Mom whacked him in the chest lightly with her gloved hand.

"Oh, stop, you two," she said. "It's not that bad."

I smiled at her. "That's exactly what Missouri said."

"And she's right, as always," Mom retorted.

"Yup," I replied with a smirk, "women always are. Right, Dad?"

Dad nodded solemnly, a smile playing at his lips as he side-eyed Mom.

Mom ignored his witty look, speaking to me instead. "What are you and Missouri going to do now?"

"I don't know. Might just drop her off at home. I still have work tomorrow."

The temperature was dropping, and with the sun having been down for a few hours already, it felt much later than it was.

"Alright, sweetheart," Mom said as she reached over the short wall to give me a hug. "We'll see you on Thursday night for dinner."

Dad waved, and I said goodbye before walking back to the tables near the concession stand. Missouri sat with her mom and dad, laughing and smiling. It warmed my heart to see her laughing with her dad after talking through what bothered her.

I didn't want to interrupt their family moment, but I also had to see if Missouri needed a ride home.

Her eyes met mine as I approached their table, and her smile grew, forming those little creases by her eyes that told me it was her most genuine, happy smile.

My body always filled with heat when that smile was pointed directly at me.

"Hey," she said.

The three of them watched me. I felt like they could all see right through me, straight down to my core. Like they knew every little thing I wanted to say to Missouri but hadn't had the guts to yet. Did they know all the ways I wanted to kiss her too?

I pushed the uncomfortable feelings of inadequacy and fear aside.

"I have to get going. I have work tomorrow," I said.

Mrs. Bellview gave me an empathetic look. "You don't have to work on Christmas Eve, do you?"

"No, just tomorrow. Then I have off until next week." I stretched out my back, tired and ready for the holiday vacation.

Missouri stood up from the table. "Can you drive me home?"

"Sure. I assumed you wanted a ride, but I was going to ask if you preferred your parents to drive you."

Her dad shook his head, looking at me. "No, no. You can take her. We're going to stay a while longer and hang out with Phil and Marlene. Where are they, anyway? We haven't seen them since we got off the ice for a break."

I chuckled at the picture of my dad on the ice.

"They're still out there," I said. "Mom's practically got Dad under wife arrest, so he can't leave her the whole night. And believe me, I think he's hating the ice just as much as I did."

They all laughed, and Missouri hugged her parents before we walked down the path toward the parking lot.

Chapter Thirteen

"Did you get everything sorted with your dad?" I asked once we had enough distance between us and the noisy plaza.

Missouri coughed, and her lips turned up, softening her features. "Yeah, everything's good now."

"I'm glad."

When we reached my car, I opened the passenger door. Missouri slid in, and I closed the door gently behind her. She was already removing her shoes.

I chuckled to myself, forever entertained by Missouri's adorable quirks that I loved so much.

We drove in silence while the radio played Christmas songs until I finally asked, "So, have you thought anymore about staying here?"

She knew I was referring to changing her mind on NYU. "No. I mean, yes, I have thought about it," she said seriously. "But I *have* to go. I was talking to my mom about it, trying to decide what to do. Did you know she never went to college?"

I shook my head.

Missouri let out a breath. "She told me she had the chance

to go to a great school, but then she fell in love with my dad during her senior year of high school. They got married that summer, when they were eighteen, and she got pregnant right away. Mom said she loved every minute of it, but she's always wondered what life would have been like if she had experienced college, where her life would have taken her." Her brows sank for a second, and she continued. "I don't want that to happen to me. I'll be forever wondering *what if* if I don't go to NYU. And even if I still want to teach for a while after I graduate, at least I'll have furthered my education to use later."

I pressed my lips together, nodding. "I understand." My eyes left the road for a second to take in her expression.

She was watching me, waiting for my reaction.

"I'm happy for you," I said, "just like I was when you first told me about your acceptance letter."

She relaxed into her seat, resting her feet on the dash.

"And I still want to come with you," I stated.

I thought I saw her smile, but she hid it so well that I might have imagined it.

With her head pushed back against the headrest, she turned her face toward me. "You do realize that I'll be busy, like, *all the time*, right?"

I hummed an acknowledgement.

"And I can't be spending all my free time at your apartment or wherever you decide to live. Things won't be the same as here."

"I know."

"Then how do you know you'll want it—that life?" Her voice was so quiet I almost missed it.

My brows pulled down, and I assessed her face for a second before returning my attention to the road. I reached out and grabbed her hand, threading our fingers together in a more intimate way than we'd ever done before.

"Because I just want you. It doesn't matter what we're doing, where we are, or how much time we get to spend together. I just want you. Even if it's in tiny increments. I'll take anything. I'd rather get five minutes *with* you than have a whole day without you at all."

"Really?" She rubbed at her nose with the back of her sleeve, sniffing gently.

"Really." I continued to hold her hand as I drove. "So, is that a *yes* to me coming with you?"

She moved our joined hands closer, pressing her other hand over them like she was afraid I'd disappear. "It's still a *maybe*."

I raised a brow and tilted my head to catch her eye. "A *maybe* that's sort of like a *yes*?"

"Maybe," she repeated, a smile playing in her voice.

I walked her to her door when we got to her apartment. She invited me in, but I had to say no, knowing if I did I'd leave much later than I should.

Only a single day of work sat between me and a four-day holiday weekend spent entirely with her.

Lampposts in the parking lot glimmered dimly over her blonde hair, tinting it bronze, while shadows covered her face. Missouri looked tired as we stood outside her door, and she rubbed at her eyes, then sniffed.

I looked her over while she unlocked her door. "Are you feeling okay?"

"Yup, I'm fine," she said. "I'm just kind of tired from skating, I guess."

"Come here." I pulled her into a hug, and she slowly fell into me like she had been waiting for this moment all night.

My body relaxed as I wrapped her in my arms. She was my safe space. My home.

With the way I felt about her, we could make distance work. I could stay here and wait for her to complete her master's degree. I was willing to have a long-distance relationship if it meant being with her.

But I was letting her make the choice for the both of us. I'd understood my true feelings for a long time, but for her it was all new. So I couldn't blame her for being uncertain about this next step.

The one that I wanted to take *so* badly.

Her arms squeezed tight around my middle. I moved my hands to her cheeks and tilted her face up to mine. Her body leaned into me, and the fog between our breaths grew. Her eyes closed in anticipation, and I pressed my lips gently to her forehead.

Her skin was warm, contrasting with the chill in the air. When I pulled away, she looked up at me with what looked like desire in her eyes.

"Good night, Missouri," I murmured softly.

I opened the door for her, and she stepped inside, watching me as I walked away.

Her voice followed me on the chilly breeze, filling me with longing. "Good night, Jacob."

The day before Christmas Eve, I worked a full day and then stopped at my parents' house before heading home. A mug of hot tea rested in front of me, and Purrseus sat on my lap at the kitchen counter, his large body looking even bigger from this angle.

Mom pushed a plate of homemade pastries toward me,

and I grabbed a glorious-looking orange scone. On the first bite, my mouth exploded with flavor.

"Mom, these are amazing," I said, taking a second, much larger bite. "I wish you had made these when I was a kid. I could have lived off these."

"You can take some home with you. Have them tomorrow for breakfast." She stepped around the counter and sat on the wooden stool next to me, her own mug of tea in hand. "So what brings you here after work? I didn't expect to see you until tomorrow for the movie night."

I finished off the scone on the third bite and took a sip of my tea. "I wanted to talk to you about Missouri and NYU."

She watched me without blinking as she nodded. "It's pretty far from Nebraska, isn't it?"

"It is." I wrapped my hands around the hot mug. The heat grounded me, forcing me to tell my mom what was on my mind. It was the reason I had come here, but it was still hard for me to be vulnerable. "I want to go with her to New York. Do you think that's crazy? Is it a bad idea?"

Mom's eyes didn't leave mine as she replied, "It's not crazy at all. In fact, it's exactly what I thought you'd do."

"You knew I'd want to follow her?" I frowned.

"I knew you wouldn't want to be without her."

I nodded, watching the minty teabag float in my cup.

"What has she said about you going with her?" she asked.

I shrugged. "She doesn't want me to uproot my life for her." I looked at Mom. "But I told her how I feel about her."

Mom raised her brows. "That's a big move. Did she say how she felt about that?"

I stroked Purrseus's long fur, and he purred, nuzzling his nose into my hand every time I pulled it away. I was beginning to feel like the cat, chasing Missouri every time she wasn't around.

But I couldn't help it. I wanted everything she could give me.

"She didn't really say how she felt, other than over-whelmed. There are a lot of things changing for her right now, with school and moving, quitting her job. She said she wants to go slow."

Mom smiled. "Slow might be hard, considering you've been together almost every day since the day you were born."

I gave her a half smile. "That was my thought too. But if I can just go with her to New York, we can wait to put a label on it. We can continue just how we've always been until she feels settled and ready to move forward."

Mom sipped her tea, biding her time before she made a comment. When she finally spoke, she looked wiser, her demeanor both relaxed and confident.

"I think moving to New York is a good idea," she said. "Missouri will need someone familiar in a big city like that, even if she doesn't realize it yet." She leaned back a little. "And it will be good for both of you to figure out life together somewhere new. Being so far out of your comfort zone can change you, and it's important to see how you work together to overcome the big changes."

I contemplated her words as I took another scone, this time eating it in two bites. "Yeah," I nodded, feeling better. "That makes sense. We've always seen each other in the same light, hung out with the same friends and family. You're right. It will be good for us to have a new setting."

Mom's short brown hair swayed as she nodded. "Is anything else bothering you?" she asked before draining her mug. "You know I love talking with you about anything." Her smile was bright, and it chased away my fears, just as it had always chased away nighttime shadows when I was a kid.

"No, nothing else."

She put her hand on my back. "It will all turn out the way it's supposed to. You're both smart. I know you'll make the right choice for both of you. Just give her the space she needs when she asks for it. If there's one thing that will scare a girl away, it's making her feel like there's only one choice—one that's too big and scary to commit to."

"Okay." I gave Mom a hug, and Purrseus jumped off my lap. "Thanks, Mom. I needed to talk it through, but I didn't think Mark would be the right person for this one."

Mom laughed. "No, Mark is probably too blunt to give you the time you need to process all the possibilities."

I stood, ready to head home and call Missouri. Mom put a few scones in a bag for me and walked me to the door.

"Just don't ever leave her questioning how you feel," she said. "Lay it all out as much as you can. Be honest, and let her talk through her fears, just like you did with me." She hugged me again, and I thanked her for the scones and the advice.

When I stepped out the door, I couldn't wait any longer to hear Missouri's voice. I immediately called her while setting the bag of pastries on the passenger seat.

When she answered, her voice was hoarse. "Hello?"

"Hey, you don't sound right. Are you okay?" I started the engine.

"I have a little cold. Nothing major, though. I'm okay." She coughed, and her voice was muffled.

"You don't sound okay," I said. "I'm coming over. I'll bring you medicine." I was already pulling out of the driveway in the direction of her apartment.

"No, Jacob. Don't come over. I don't want to get you sick."

Her voice was so small and pathetic; it made me want to take care of her more.

"I'll be fine. Do you have tissues?" I asked, thinking of all the supplies she would need.

"I have toilet paper."

"I'll get you tissues." I added it to my mental list of things to get at the pharmacy. "What about soup?"

"Yeah, I just had some SpaghettiOs." Muffled sounds came through my phone again, followed by a fit of coughs.

"SpaghettiOs are delicious, I'll give you that, Missouri. But they don't count as soup when you're sick."

There was silence on the line, and I imagined her rolling her eyes at me.

I pulled into the nearest pharmacy parking lot. "I'll be there in fifteen minutes."

Missouri let me into her apartment, and I entered holding two plastic bags.

Her hair was loose and knotted, and she wore a matching plaid Christmas pajama set in forest green. The pants hung a little too long past her feet, and she pulled the sleeves over her hands to cover them.

"You don't look so good," I said, taking note of the bags under her eyes.

"Wow, thanks." She rolled her eyes. "That's exactly what I was hoping you'd say."

She followed me to the kitchen as I laid the bags on the counter, pulling items out and placing them in front of her.

"Tissues, Advil, soup, Gatorade, crackers, and liquid cold medicine." I listed off the items as I showed them to her. "And cough drops. You like the cherry ones, right?"

Missouri stared at me, then nodded.

"Good," I said. "What are your symptoms?"

"Um… coughing. And I have a headache and a runny nose."

"Then I got you just the right thing." I opened the bottle of liquid cold medicine and poured some into the little measuring cup that came with it. "Here, take this."

She took the tiny cup and downed the red liquid.

Putting a hand on her back, I guided her to the living room. "I'll make you some soup," I said. "You should just rest."

"Jacob, I'm okay," she said weakly. "You don't have to do all this."

She reluctantly lay on the couch, and I draped a blanket over her body. The lights on the Christmas tree weren't on, so I plugged them in and turned on the TV.

"Are the lights okay, or do you want them off?"

She smiled up at me, her cheeks flushed red from her cold. "The lights are cozy. I like them."

I checked her head for fever with the back of my hand. She was a little warm but not burning up. The medicine would help keep a fever at bay.

I handed her the TV remote and returned to the kitchen to make her a can of chicken noodle soup. I would have loved to make it homemade, but I couldn't make her wait that long.

When the soup boiled, I ladled it into a large snowflake mug and brought it to her.

She sat up, taking the hot mug from my hands. "Thank you. You didn't have to come here and make a fuss over me. It's just a little cold. I'll be better by tomorrow."

"I'll always fuss over you," I said, meaning it.

Our eyes met, and her warm smile made my heart dive deep into my stomach. It amazed me that I'd known her my entire life, and yet I still had these physical reactions to her.

Every time I looked at her, my brain experienced a cosmic shift, like it was the first time I'd ever laid eyes on her.

Even when she was sick and felt terrible, she was still the most beautiful woman I'd ever seen.

"Sit down," she said, motioning me over. "We can both fit. Let's watch a holiday rom-com."

Missouri pulled her feet back, making room for me, and I sat on the other end of the loveseat. I lifted her feet and rested them on my lap, covering them with her blanket. She held the cup of soup carefully to keep it from spilling as she moved.

"Is this okay?" I asked.

She nodded. "Yes, that's okay." She averted her eyes, suddenly finding the commercial on TV to be very interesting.

She scanned through the movies on her streaming platform and ultimately landed on a Christmas romance she'd watched over a hundred times before. It was her comfort movie. It warmed my heart to see her pick this one when she was sick because I knew it would help her feel better. Nostalgia was great medicine.

Missouri ate her soup, and I rested my hands on her shins as the movie began.

She fell asleep halfway through, but I stayed. I let her sleep, and I eventually fell asleep too with her feet draped across my legs and her smile playing across my dreams.

Chapter Fourteen

"Jacob?" Someone was shaking my arm. "Jacob, wake up." Missouri's angelic voice cut through my dreams, and the warmth of her hand on my shoulder stirred me back to reality.

I opened my eyes and was met with my best friend's beautiful face, her eyes bright in the morning light.

I sat up, taking note of the sun shining through the window and the rows of snow globes on the shelves nearby. "Did I fall asleep? Are you okay?"

"I'm fine." She sat back against a pillow. Her legs were no longer resting over mine, and my neck felt stiff. "You slept here all night," she said sympathetically.

"Yeah," I rubbed at the back of my neck, rolling my head to the side. "It feels like it."

She sat on her hands, tucking her knees up to her chin as she watched me. "You didn't have to stay."

"I know, but I didn't want to leave you." I kept my eyes on hers, and her warm smile lit me up like a Christmas tree. After a second, I pressed the back of my fingers to her forehead. "No fever. Do you feel better?"

"I feel great. Must have been a twenty-four-hour thing. Thank you for coming over last night." She grinned. "Merry Christmas Eve."

"Merry Christmas Eve," I said, smiling too. Then I frowned. "Wait. That didn't count as our Christmas Eve movie night, did it?"

"No," she laughed, the sound ringing in my ears like the merriest of Christmas bells. "I was sick, and yesterday wasn't even Christmas Eve yet." She ran a hand through her long knotted hair, looking as beautiful as ever.

"Good." My shoulders relaxed. "Because you were asleep for most of it."

"And it was the best night's sleep I think I've ever had," she replied, her cheeks turning a light shade of pink.

Besides the blush in her cheeks, she looked relatively healthy again, back to her normal glow.

"I'll make you some tea," I said, standing and stretching out my aching muscles.

"I need to shower first," she replied, folding the blanket I had draped over her last night. "I feel so gross after being sick. I'll take a quick shower and be out in a few minutes."

She paused thoughtfully before adding, "You don't have to stay. I'll see you later anyway at your parents' house." Her eyes met mine expectantly as she waited for my response.

"I'll stay."

A smile stretched over her face, and she bit her lip. "Okay." She beamed. "I'll be right back."

She scampered down the hall, and I grabbed a mug for her tea.

❄

Throughout the morning, Missouri and I played a few board games, watched episodes of her favorite sitcom, and ate a lunch that I ordered and had delivered to her apartment. This Christmas Eve had already started out to be a warm and cozy day, and I looked forward to our family dinner tonight.

Eventually, I decided it was time for me to go home. I'd see her again in just a few short hours, but I struggled anyway to get myself out the door.

"Are you sure you're feeling better?" I asked, standing with my hand on the doorknob.

It was obvious that she was back to normal, but I couldn't help worrying about her.

She nodded. "Yes. I'm fine, thanks to you. I'm feeling like myself again."

Her smile practically knocked me off my feet. Her hair was wavy after drying naturally, and she'd gotten dressed in black leggings and an oversized light blue knit sweater stitched with silver snowflakes. It made the color of her eyes pop.

"Alright. I'll see you tonight." My brain told me to step out the door, but my heart pulled me back to her.

She seemed to feel the tug, and she stepped into my arms. They wrapped protectively around her, and I was filled with a sense of purpose when she came near, like holding her was my whole reason for being.

I forced myself to let her go, leaving before the invisible ribbon between us could pull me to her so hard that my lips crashed into hers.

When I walked into my parents' house, I was greeted by absolutely no one. I frowned because I was usually bombarded by the whole crew of parents when I arrived.

Rockin' Around the Christmas Tree was playing from the kitchen, and voices rang out from that direction. Dad and Brad sounded like they were talking about football, while Missouri's voice chimed over the laughter of both our moms.

I kicked off my shoes by the door and hung my coat on a hook on the wall. The sound of a tiny bell reached my ears, and I looked down to see Purrseus rounding the corner. His big gray body waddled toward me, and his tail swooshed gracefully from side to side. When he reached me, his body pressed against my legs, and he meowed dramatically, looking for attention.

I picked him up.

"Hey, boy," I said, snuggling my face into his long hair. He purred, and my nose brushed against something around his neck. I pulled back to find a thin green ribbon tied loosely there, a tiny silver bell dangling from it.

I rolled my eyes and chuckled to myself. This had Missouri written all over it.

Then lo and behold, Missouri rounded the same corner, her socks sliding on the hardwood floor. When she looked up and saw me, her lips pulled into a wide smile, her white teeth shining.

"You're here!" she sang cheerfully.

"What is this on Purrseus's neck?"

"Oh," she giggled, "that's his Christmas present!"

My brow lifted. "What if he suffocates?"

"What if he suffocates?" she said in a mocking voice, a smile twisting on her lips. She stretched out her arms and took him, leaving me empty-handed.

I frowned.

"He'll be fine," she said placatingly. "It's not tight at all. You're such a cat daddy."

The corner of my mouth quirked up at the name. "A cat daddy? I like the sound of that."

She blushed, but she didn't hide it this time, keeping her wide eyes on mine.

"What?" I asked when she didn't stop staring at me.

"You've been flirting with me. A lot," she accused.

I stepped closer to her. "Is that okay?"

When I took another step closer, she didn't back down.

"Actually," she said, breathless. "I think I kind of like it."

"That's good to know," I breathed.

I pet Purrseus, allowing my hand to brush over Missouri's. Her skin singed mine, and I reveled in the heat of her soft skin.

"Oh, you're here!" Dad walked into the entryway, and I dropped my hand.

"Hey, Dad." I gave him a hug.

"Dinner is ready. Come on," he said, leading us into the kitchen where everyone else was waiting.

I said hi to everyone, and when Mom called us all to the table, we followed her into the dining room.

The Christmas Eve dinner spread was immaculate. A large sliced ham rested on a holiday platter, and a carved turkey sat beside a huge bowl of mouthwatering mashed potatoes. There were bowls of gravy and stuffing, cranberry sauce, Mom's homemade dinner rolls in a basket, and Mrs. Bellview's famous homemade cinnamon applesauce—which I planned to heavily indulge in.

I stood behind Missouri. "Did you write the name tags?" I whispered over her shoulder. Each spot at the table had a white cardstock name tag written on in clean cursive.

I felt, more than saw, her smile. "Yes. Your mom insisted I not make any of the food—her loss."

I chuckled at the sentiment.

"So, I set the table and made it look fancy," she shrugged.

"Oh yeah, very fancy."

She elbowed me in my stomach, and I laughed, stepping back from her dangerous arms.

"Everyone has an assigned seat this year, thanks to Missouri and her beautiful place settings," Mom announced to our small group.

We all found our names and took our seats.

Amusingly, we were all in the same places we normally sat. No one commented on it, but I resolved to make fun of Missouri and her aversion to change later.

Chatter erupted in waves as we ate, and we took only a few moments between conversations to stuff our faces with all the amazing food.

When our bellies were full, there were plenty of leftovers. Missouri and I packed away what was left of the meal, dividing it between the Bellviews and Kleins so everyone had plenty to save for a meal later.

"Are you sure you don't want to come with us to see *Christmas All the Way*?" Missouri's mom asked us as they bundled up in their coats and gloves.

"No, thanks. We'll stick to the classics tonight," Missouri answered, hugging her mom and dad goodbye.

"What did you pick to watch this year?" Dad asked. He had on his big coat, the one with lots of pockets.

"The Santa Clause," we answered in unison. Missouri stuck out her tongue at me, and I sneered playfully back at her.

"Oh, that's a good one," said Mr. Bellview. "Speaking of good, Phil, did you pack the goodies?"

"Of course." Dad beamed and patted his coat pockets—all four of them.

"What are you sneaking into the theater this time?" Mom quirked a brow, and Mrs. Bellview snickered.

"Just the snacks." Putting on his nice leather gloves, Dad

pointed to each pocket. "Reese's Pieces, LIFE SAVERS Gummies, Sour Patch Kids, and Junior Mints."

I turned to Missouri. "Did you bring candies for our movie night?"

Her face fell. "No, was I supposed to?"

I pulled a bag of Skittles out of my jeans pocket and handed it to her. "Nope. I got you."

She snatched the bag from my hand. "Jacob! I really thought we forgot the candy!" She turned to my mom. "He's always teasing, Mrs. Klein. How do you put up with him?"

Mom just smiled, looking between us with a soft expression.

Dad opened the front door, ready to lead them all out. "We better get going if we want to make it on time."

The parents followed him, and soon Missouri and I were left alone.

She turned to me. "Are you ready for Christmas Eve movie night?" she asked excitedly.

"I've only waited three hundred sixty-five days for it," I said, my reply dripping with sarcasm.

Missouri laughed and ran to the living room.

I followed slowly behind, and we took our seats on the couch. Missouri was already finding the movie on the TV, and I made sure to sit closer to her than I normally would.

She either didn't notice or she didn't mind the proximity.

The living room was decorated just as it was every year for Christmas, with Mom and Dad's tall, wide Christmas tree taking up a quarter of the room. It was covered in sentimental ornaments, most of them ones my mom had collected over the years, ever since I was a baby. There was even one that said "Baby's First Christmas."

The tan L-shaped couch faced the tree, and the TV hung directly over the mantel, which was draped in holly-and-pine garland. Golden pine cones and white wooden snowflakes rested between the greenery, and the lit fireplace warmed the living room with the glow of the flames.

I smiled, knowing Dad had lit it just for us. They didn't use the fireplace often, but they knew Missouri and I loved it.

Before Missouri pressed play, I asked, "Do you want popcorn yet, or should we have an intermission to get snacks?"

"Let's wait," she said, popping a handful of Skittles into her mouth. "I'm not really hungry yet."

I eyed the bag of candy, then her.

"What?" she asked through a fruity mouthful. Her brows drew together as she assessed me.

"I just like when you're you." I smiled.

She chewed slowly, then finally swallowed the Skittles. "Who else would I be?" she questioned.

I took the remote from her, emptying her hand for the sole purpose of filling it with mine. She watched as our fingers weaved together, then her eyes found my face.

There was a moment of silence, and then she asked, "Are you sure you're ready for this?" Her eyes moved down to my lips.

"I'm ready for anything with you, Missouri." Our bodies pulled toward each other, like two boats drifting together on the sea.

The corners of her lips twitched slightly. "I was talking about the movie."

"Me too," I murmured, not at all thinking of the movie.

She was only inches from my mouth, her lips parting slightly with what could only be described as *want*.

"Do you want to kiss me?" Her voice was as quiet as a silent breeze on a winter night.

I nodded, searching her eyes.

"I want to kiss you too," she said.

And before she could even finish the last word, I was pressing my lips to hers. She wrapped her arm around my neck, and I pulled her closer until our bodies were flush against one another. She tasted like strawberry and green apple and all the colors of the rainbow.

Her chest rose as I tilted my mouth against hers. She sighed into my mouth, and her tongue found mine, making me melt into the couch.

When we finally pulled away, we were sucking in air.

"Is this slow? Like you wanted?" I asked, running my fingers through her hair and over her shoulder.

She shook her head. "No, but it's exactly how I want it."

My forehead rested against hers as she closed her eyes, and her hands framed my face in the sweetest of touches.

"Are you sure this is what you want? Us, together like this?" I asked.

She nodded against my forehead, but I shook my head.

"I need to hear you *say* it," I said. "Say you want me."

"I want you, Jacob." Her eyes opened, and I leaned back slightly to watch her face. "I want you to come to New York," she continued. "I want you to live there while I get my master's degree. And I want to spend every single second of my very limited free time with you." She smiled, and I slowly pushed my lips against hers again.

Seconds, or minutes, or hours later, we finally started the movie. Our feet touched as we rested them on the coffee table, and our hands remained linked together as if we were afraid to lose the other if we let go.

Intermission was used for getting more kisses rather than making popcorn, and I filed the night away as the best Christmas Eve movie night we'd ever had.

Chapter Fifteen

"Come on!" Missouri shouted, flashing her white smile at me through the falling snow.

She trekked through the deepening layers of snowflakes until she made it to the top of the hill. It was right down the street from my parents' house and perfect for sledding. At this early hour on Christmas morning, there was no one here but us.

Last night, I drove Missouri home when my parents got back, and then I picked her up again this morning, bringing her a large thermos of coffee and a kiss—or two or five. I was the happiest I'd ever been, all because I got to finally call her mine.

I held my own plastic sled and caught up to her.

"I'll race you," she said, resting her sled on the hilltop and climbing on.

"Loser has to wash the dishes after family breakfast?" I tossed a grin in her direction and climbed into my sled next to hers.

"Deal," she stated, readying herself. "On the count of three.

One, two—" She shoved at my sled, cackling as she raced prematurely down the hill.

"Hey!" I righted myself and followed after her.

The wind whipped through her hair as she sped down the hill in front of me. The chill stung my cheeks and burned my nose, and the snow falling down blurred the scenery all around me. All I saw was a landscape of white, with Missouri ahead of me being the only colorful thing in sight.

Catching up to her, I heard her laughter over the swooshing of the sleds. Her sled stopped, but I was still moving quickly toward her.

"Watch out!" I shouted, my sled racing nearer.

She stood up beside her sled, but I was coming in too fast.

With no time for her to jump out of the way, I grabbed her as my sled made contact with hers, pulling her onto my lap. She screamed, and we plowed into her sled, shoving it roughly aside. My sled kept gliding along the snow with her clinging to me.

Finally, the sled slowed on flat ground, and when we stopped, we were silent. The only sound was the clinking of falling snow, like tiny crystals layering themselves upon one another. It almost sounded like it was raining.

Missouri's body started shaking with bouts of laughter under my arms, which were wrapped loosely around her waist. She tipped sideways, slipping off my lap and tumbling into the snow, cackling and breathless.

I smiled, watching her with amusement.

"You almost killed me," she wheezed, rolling onto her back.

"You cheated," I reminded her.

She hummed a sound of agreement. "That is absolutely true, I did cheat. But"—she held a pointer finger in the air—"I *won*. So it was totally worth it."

"You're ridiculous." I threw a snowball at her, hitting her in the arm, which made her produce another excited scream.

She scrambled to her feet, frantically making snowballs and throwing them at me. One hit me in the head, covering my beanie and part of my face in snow.

She gasped, holding her hands over her mouth in shock. "Oops. I'm so sorry, I didn't mean for that to—"

I stood slowly, allowing the snow to fall dramatically off my face, and she went still. The snow was cold as it stuck to my eyelashes and melted on my nose.

Missouri backed away, her face becoming serious. "Jacob," she said, "what're you doing?"

I stalked toward her, like a snow cat ready to pounce, and she began to run.

I chased after her and caught her easily.

Grabbing the sleeve of her jacket, I swung her around until she was in my arms, her face just inches from mine. Her laughter was music to my ears, and I buried my cold face in her neck.

The sounds of our heavy breaths mingled with the soft fall of the snow, forming a delicate bubble of the universe that was all ours. The fog from our warm breaths mingled in the frosty air, and snowflakes fell on her cheeks as her face turned up to mine. This close, I could see the individual flakes and the intricate designs that made up each one as they landed on her eyelashes.

Her eyes scanned mine, shifting from right to left, and when her eyes dipped to my lips, I pulled her closer, wrapping my arms tighter around her waist. She leaned into me, her arms draped around my neck, her face so close to mine that I felt the tickle of snowflakes on her nose as it brushed against mine.

"It's taken me a while to admit it to myself," she said quietly, "because I was scared that change would be too hard to manage, but... I think deep down, I always knew I wanted you, Jacob."

I tilted my head to look at her. "You've always wanted me? Since when?"

She giggled when I squeezed her tighter. "I think since the first time we ever went ice skating together."

My brows pulled down. "Why? I was falling all over the place. It definitely wasn't my best look. I was so embarrassed."

"That's exactly why."

I raised a brow in question.

"I knew you weren't enjoying it, but you stuck it out for me because you knew I loved ice skating. And it was then that I started to see you were always doing things for me. You're selfless. You take care of me. You're always making me happy." She stood on her toes, pulling me closer to her. "You've always been it for me."

I leaned down and kissed her with everything in me. We made up for all the years we missed, the years we floated through life on a level of friendship that should have been so much more the whole time. I felt her remove her gloves behind me, and then she ran her fingers through my damp hair at the base of my neck.

Smiling against her lips, I slid my hand behind her head, pulling her face nearer to me. The world slowed. The sun shone down in a wintery veil, making the snow shine all around us, and I became lost in this moment. We were in our own little snow globe, surrounded by sparkly white snow and seeing my dream come true.

We pulled away, taking a second to breathe, and she laughed happily. "I can't believe this," she said.

I removed my gloves with my teeth so I could feel her skin against my hand, and pressed my palm against her cheek. She leaned her face into it. "Believe what?" I asked.

"This. Us." She stared into my eyes, then frowned, the crease between her brows deepening. "What if this changes us?"

I shook my head. "It won't. Nothing can change us."

"But how do you know?"

"Because we'll always be us. Missouri and Jacob. We're tied to one another, whether or not we comprehend the hows and the whys. I always knew it was written in our stars that we'd be together forever. I just couldn't have dreamed that all those nights in the backyard, wishing with you upon shooting stars, would one day make you mine."

She blinked away a snowflake on her lashes. "Is that what you always wished for?"

"Well,"—I nodded my head back and forth in contemplation—"at least since I was twelve."

"The year you got Purrseus?" she asked.

I pulled her closer, and she placed her hands on both sides of my neck, just under my ears. Her fingers were cold against my skin, but not unwelcome.

"Exactly," I said. "I wished that we would both get pets. But then, I was the one who got one, and you didn't. So I believed that he was *our* cat."

Her face scrunched like she was about to cry.

"The day I got him, it felt like he was for both of us," I continued. "You were so in love with him, you cried and you looked beautiful, even at twelve years old. I felt myself falling in love with you in that moment."

Her eyes grew wide at the mention of love, and she moved her hands to my chest. "So if you never got Purrseus, you wouldn't have fallen in love with me?"

Her playful smile made me want to pinch her side and tickle her, but I held her tight. "There were plenty of other moments that I fell in love with you. It would take forever to list them all."

"We'll have plenty of time in the future then," she said smoothly. "Will you be okay living in New York?"

"Missouri," I held her hands in mine. "I'll be okay as long as I'm wherever you are. We'll figure it out."

"Are you sure?"

"More sure than I've ever been about anything, besides that I love you."

Her eyes flew to mine. "Say that again."

I brought her hand up between us and kissed her fingers. "I love you."

Her smile lit up the already impossibly bright morning, and I could no longer feel the cold.

She stared into my eyes with more adoration than I could ever hope for. "I love you too, Jacob."

I kissed her deeply once again, until I felt dizzy on her love.

And when we came up for air, she smiled and whispered, "Merry Christmas, Jacob. And happy birthday."

I whispered into her ear in return, "Do you want your present right now?"

She frowned. "You have it out here? In the snow?"

I opened the zippered pocket on my coat and pulled out a small wrapped gift. Missouri took it in her hands, her eyes delighted.

"Go ahead. Open it," I said, watching the smile on her face grow.

She pulled on the little red bow and ripped apart the white wrapping paper.

I gathered the paper from her hands and stuffed it in my pocket.

When she saw a jewelry box, she frowned. "Jacob…"

"It's not a ring," I reassured her. "I thought you wouldn't say yes if I proposed this early into our official relationship."

Her lips turned up, and she laughed. "You weren't wrong."

She opened the box, and her eyes bounced back to mine in surprise.

"This is the tiniest snow globe I've ever seen." She lifted the snow globe between her fingers, delicately removing it from the box.

A small gold chain followed, linked to the snow globe to create an elegant necklace.

"So now you can take one with you everywhere and wear it all year." I pointed to the snow globe. "It's me and you at the Statue of Liberty. It's just one of the many things I plan to do with you in New York. I know I usually get you a snow globe that commemorates our past year, but this one is to celebrate our future."

She held it close to her eyes to better see the intricate details, and her smile widened. "It's perfect."

Turning around, she let me clasp it around her neck. It rested just above her heart. Not yet having taken her eyes off it, she looked up at me. "It's beautiful, Jacob. I love it so much."

My lungs expanded, and my breath caught. It meant the world to me that she liked it.

"Merry Christmas, Missouri. Happy birthday." I pressed my lips to hers, thinking I could never get enough of my best friend.

The snow continued to fall, swirling around our bodies and pressing us together.

If I could have created a snow globe large enough to hold all of my most perfect moments, I would have pressed this one into it. It would be a snow globe overflowing with happy memories. They would all include Missouri, my best friend and the love of my life, the one who's been beside me since day one.

Acknowledgments

As always, I need to first say thank you to my Savior for saving me. He continues to make this writing journey possible. Thank you, Lord, for loving me, a sinner, and for giving me a place to write love stories. His love for me (and you, dear reader) is the greatest love story ever told.

Thank you to my beta readers, Jordy, Shelby, and Tatum. You're all so generous with your time, and you're each an amazing cheerleader for indie authors like myself. Without your input and time, this story would not have been completed before Christmas. Thank you from the bottom of my heart.

Cheyenne, you're the best! Thank you for helping me with my first Christmas novella. Your input and editing was amazing, and your willingness to do this with short notice meant everything.

Alicia, thank you for being such a great proofreader! As this story was a last minute project for me, I appreciate you taking it on as soon as you could. And your encouragement and kind words about my novella mean the world to me! It's because of you that I've been able to polish Since Day One until it shined.

And thank you to all my readers! Whether this is the first book of mine that you're reading, or if you've been with me since the beginning when I released Meeting Me, Loving You, I'm grateful that you're here. Without readers like you, I wouldn't be able to do this.

Also by Abigail Nadine

Meeting Me, Loving You

About the Author

Abigail Nadine learned of her love for reading in the early years of middle school, but never imagined she'd write a book of her own. She graduated in 2016 with two Bachelor's of Science degrees in math and science education, then worked as an ophthalmic technician for several years. Although she doesn't teach in the classroom or work in the medical field now, she enjoys reading and writing about those who do. Originally from Pennsylvania, she began writing in 2024 after moving to Kansas with her husband and two children.

Abigail is an author of swoon-filled, closed-door romance books that are full of heart, struggle, and happily ever afters. When she's not writing, she can most likely be found reading a romance or fantasy book, sipping coffee, playing with her kids, cuddling her dog, Calvin, and most certainly always avoiding the laundry.

instagram.com/abigailnadine.author

amazon.com/Meeting-Loving-Hearts-Maple-Lake-%20e-book/dp/B0DK2914PL?ref_=ast_author_mpb

Scan the QR code below to connect with Abigail and leave a review.